Every White Man's Fantasy

Also by Linda Porter Harrison

Torn Between 2 Brothas

Think Like a Man
and here's a thought: Start
Acting Like a Man

The 25 mistakes men make that prevent them
from finding and keeping true love

Stuck on Stupid or Stuck in Stupid

The 25 mistakes women make that prevent
them from attracting and keeping real love

Every White Man's Fantasy

LINDA PORTER HARRISON

authorHOUSE®

AuthorHouse™
1663 Liberty Drive
Bloomington, IN 47403
www.authorhouse.com
Phone: 1 (800) 839-8640

Published by AuthorHouse 11/17/2015

ISBN: 978-1-5049-5751-9 (sc)
ISBN: 978-1-5049-5750-2 (e)

Print information available on the last page.

"APPETIZER"

WILLIAM GALLANTINE

Now, some of ya'll out there is gonna get real upset about what I have to say. Shoot. I ain't never really cared about what folk thought about me and the day that I do, I'll probably roll over and die. See, I'm one of the richest men in the state of Tennessee and I didn't get this way caring what folk thought. I do what I want, when I want to do it. I've always been my own man. Now, I wanna talk about a subject matter that makes plenty folks uncomfortable. You ready? Alright, if you say so. Every white man in America longs for a piece and a taste of black pussy. Period. Don't cover your mouth acting like you all shocked, because everybody knows it's true. Now we, I mean white folk, don't discuss it all out in public. But it's a known fact that black pussy is the best damn pussy on this earth. No offense to white women, Chinese women or Mexican women, but black women just know what to do.

Now, I'm gonna be honest with ya, I had my first taste when I was about fifteen years old. I can remember it as if it were yesterday. Her name was Helen and she was our maid. Helen couldn't have been more than seventeen. Boy, was she beautiful. She had skin the color of butterscotch and let me tell ya, it was softer than a baby's bottom. Oh, but what I miss is how Helen smelled. She smelled sweet, like the aroma from sugar cookies coming out of an oven. She even tasted sweet. Oh, I miss Helen. Now, Helen lived with my family for years. Rumor has it that she was the niece of our first maid, Miss Gloria, and that Daddy hired her on as a favor to Miss Gloria after Mama put Miss Gloria out. See, Daddy used to visit Miss Gloria's room almost every night after we all were put to bed. He and Mama used to get into some horrible confrontations about Miss Gloria, until one day Mama said that she was leaving and that Daddy had to make a choice. Either Miss Gloria left, or she was taking us and leaving. Needless to say, Miss Gloria left, but not without one request. She asked Daddy if her only niece could be hired on. Daddy made arrangements and Helen arrived the next day. Mama wasn't too happy, but she didn't make that much of a fuss.

Anyway, I used to hear my Daddy talking with my uncles and a few of his friends about Miss Gloria and how much he loved her, but because of the times he could never marry a nigger woman. He bragged about their intimate moments. Seems like everyone participating in the conversation had a woman like Miss Gloria on the side. Well, one night Daddy called me out on the porch and told me that I was about to become a real man. Everyone started laughing. And I started laughing, too. Not because I found something funny, but because I knew what was about to happen. Daddy had been hinting around for months about me needing to know how to please a woman. So, I knew what he meant when he said I was about to become a real man. I stuck my hands in my pockets out of nervousness and lowered my eyes. Daddy handed me a shot glass and told me to swallow fast…that it

4

would calm me. I grabbed the glass and quickly drank the brown liquid. It burned like hell, but soon afterwards I felt all warm and cozy on the inside. Daddy told me to head on back to the maid's quarters and that someone would be waiting for me. I hesitated and then I felt one of my uncles nudging me off the porch. "Go on, boy!" Everyone yelled. "Don't be scared, it's just like riding a bike!" The laughter got louder. I gave everyone one last look and ran towards the back of the house. When I got to the door I must have stood there for an hour, at least that's what it felt like. I was so nervous.

Finally, I knocked and Helen opened the door wearing the prettiest white gown I had ever seen. It was sorta sheer and I could see her brown nipples poking through. Boy, I got excited and felt my nature rising to full attention. Helen gestured for me to come inside and sit on the bed. I sat down and started fidgeting with my hands. It seemed like the logical thing to do. Helen grabbed my hands, placed them at my side and began undressing me. She never said a word, she just hummed a slow, bluesy tune. After I was completely naked, Helen led me to a tub of water near the fireplace and bathed me. Shoot, I had never been naked in front of a woman before…except Mama. Plus, I kept trying to cover Ol' Baxter up, but Helen would just move my hand and gently massage Ol' Baxter.

Boy I tell ya, Ol' Baxter never knew a woman's touch could feel so good. After Helen finished bathing me and handed me a towel to dry off. I heard her walking towards the bed. When I looked in her direction she had slipped out of her gown and I tell you …I truly understood what the word beautiful meant. I had never seen skin so pretty, or a figure like that. Lawd have mercy, it ain't nothing like bestowing your eyes on a black woman's ass for the first time. And when Helen guided my hands to touch her ass… ooooh wee! Heaven…simply heaven.

VICTORIA GALLANTINE

I was the most sought after woman in Nashville, and I knew it. From as far back as I can remember people have always referred to me as a "real looker." I'm tall, thin, and naturally blond with eyes bluer than the sky. I have always turned heads and knew that I could have just about any man that I set my eyes on. My daddy was Forrest Smith, the former Governor of Tennessee. Daddy was a part of the old boy network and had basically hand-picked my husband-to-be. Daddy had sworn that all of his daughters would marry money. I was all set to marry Seth Stephanow, the son of Judge George Stephanow. Seth had one of the largest law firms in Nashville. Boy, did he court me. When he proposed to me with a ten carat engagement ring; I couldn't resist. I've always had a weakness for diamonds. Well, one day Seth said he had a surprise for me. We jumped into his convertible and drove out to Belle Meade where we pulled up to a site where an enormous home was being built. We got out of the car, made our way through the rubble and stepped inside the front door.

Even though the home wasn't finished, you could tell that it was going to be fabulous. "Muffin,"…that's what Seth called me, "this is going to be our home once we're married!"

I couldn't believe it! I was so happy! My life was going just the way Daddy had planned. Grow up, attend college, marry rich, have some babies and live happily ever after…the love will come later. Don't get me wrong, I did love Seth… but he just didn't move me. I didn't get goose bumps when he touched me or all mushy on the inside. But, he was a good man and he loved me, and that was most important.

Rule #1: Always, always, marry a man that loves you more…period.

Shit, that's the one rule I never should have compromised on. After I kissed Seth and thanked him for our lovely home we decided to take a tour. While we were inspecting the kitchen, a tall, absolutely gorgeous specimen of a man walked in wearing tattered blue jeans, a white t-shirt and cowboy boots. He and Seth greeted each other and shook hands. "Victoria, this is William Gallantine, our contractor." I instantly recognized the name.

He was the largest builder in Tennessee, but I had never made his acquaintance. When he said hello, and looked into my eyes, something powerful went through me. To this day I cannot explain it. Anyway, the next day I drove myself out to the house and William was there alone. He seduced me on the same kitchen floor where our eyes locked. I went back every day until we had christened every room. I couldn't get enough of him. Two weeks before my wedding, I told Seth that I couldn't marry him. William and I caught a plane to Las Vegas and eloped. Now, being quite the socialite, I knew a little bit about everybody who was anybody. I had heard rumors about the Gallantine men and how they liked to dabble with nigger women, but I knew that once William had a taste of me, he would never…ever…ever look at another woman ever, again. What could he possibly want with another woman? Boy, was I wrong. Once we got married, every Friday he left home and went to North Nashville, where he ate dinner and screwed his nigger whore. Yes, I knew about her and yes, it bothered me at first, but I had the name, the money and the lifestyle. She could never take that away from me. Now, some twenty-plus years later, some half-educated jigga boo thinks that she is going to be with my son. Hell no! Over my dead body. And you can bet your last bottom dollar on that.

WALTER JAMES

I cannot, for life of me, describe how I am feeling right now. To say that I am pissed off would be an absolute understatement. How could she do it? How could my baby girl walk into my house with a cracker ass white boy? What the hell is she thinking? Shit, she ain't thinking. We live in Nashville, Tennessee, home of the Tennessee Titans, Meharry Medical College, Tennessee State Univeristy and Fisk…all of these educated, prominent, smart, well-off black brothers to choose from and she shows up at my house with a cracker. Well, I'll be goddamned! Oh yes, I'm mad as hell and I don't care who knows it. After everything that her mother and I have gone through. All the racism, sexism, blatant mistreatment at the hands of white folk…to come to my house with nothing but a brother is a slap in my face. Let me tell you how I really feel. If I could, I'd ship all of their cracker asses back to the Motherland and make them slave for my brothers and sisters for nearly three hundred years. I'd make them sleep on the ground, beat them whenever the mood struck, feed them leftover pig slop, and make them eat it every day for years. Then wonder why high blood pressure and high cholesterol runs rapid in their community. I'd let the brothers rape their wives and daughters in front of them and if any man tried to protect his family…they'd be lynched. I'd make them clean the house and take care of the babies so my wife could attend social events and sip tea with her associates. I have worked too hard to make sure that my baby girl has the upper hand, because I have been through hell at the hands of white people. Every time I have tried to accomplish anything, they have tried to stop me. I have been fighting all of my life. It doesn't matter that I graduated in the top one-percent of my class or that I have a PhD from Harvard. I am always being tested. My intelligence is always being questioned. Every day, some white boy tries to make me feel inadequate, or as if I'm one of the few select black men that have made it in America through affirmative action. Listen up, America ain't got time for weak brothers. We have to be strong to take the beatings that we get everyday. I'm just tired…and I just want more for my daughter. Spit on them white ass crackers. I hate them, and I'll be damned if I let some honky, rich white boy fulfill his deep-seeded fantasy with my baby girl. Hell no, it ain't gonna happen!

WILHEMENIA JAMES

I know that Walter is hurt. He's always wanted the very best for his baby girl. The best homes, the best schools, the best clothes, the best exposure to culture...just the best. Lord knows he would give his last to Willow. We tried for ten years to get pregnant without any luck. I had just about given up when one morning I felt a little light-headed when I got out of bed. I didn't feel like myself all day. This feeling lasted for a few days until I couldn't take it any more. I called my doctor and told him that he had to see me because I thought I was coming down with the flu. Boy, was I surprised when he came back into the room and said that I wasn't coming down with the flu; I was pregnant. You could have knocked me over with a feather. Seven months later we welcomed our Willow into this world. Walter and I were the happiest parents ever. Our baby has brought so much sunshine into our lives. She is bright, beautiful and has the warmest personality. We've never had any problems out of Willow. She's always been a good girl. Now, don't get me wrong; we went through all of the teenage drama and the dating years, but overall she has been a jewel. Willow has dated a few guys, some we liked and some were not worth ten cents. Her father and I agreed that we would let her find her balance when it came to dating, because we knew that we couldn't control who she ended up loving. But when she showed up with Rece, it took everything for me to keep Walter calm. He was pissed and that's putting it lightly. You have to understand, Walter went through some horrible things at the hands of white folk. We both have seen quite a bit in Nashville. This city is a far cry from where it used to be. I can't tell you how many lynchings we've seen or crosses burned. After a while you become numb, but you never forget. The memories stay embedded, deep in the back of your mind forever. Talking about it now makes me remember the sit-ins on Church Street. There's a big, beautiful library that sits there now. How ironic, a multi- million dollar building on the exact spot where white folk used to beat and spit on us. All because we wanted justice and equal rights. Let me stop talking about that period in our lives because I'll start crying. I just wanted you to have a clear picture as to why Walter cannot accept his daughter dating a white man, or "the devil", as he calls them on a good day. My Walt is something else, but he's a good man. We both want what is best for Willow. If I had my preference, Willow would marry a black man…period. No ifs, ands, or buts about it. But, it's not up to me. It's her life and after meeting Rece, I can see that he truly loves my daughter. I really can't ask for more than that. Willow is happy and that is most important. I never would have imagined a world where blacks and whites dated. I guess things have changed. Now, I just have to convince Walter to give Rece a chance. From my mouth to God's ears.

WILLOW JAMES

Men; can't live with them and can't live without them. Me, personally, I'd always choose to live with them. I simply love the company of a man, and yes, I've had my share. I don't want any regrets when I marry. I want to be sure of what I want, and how I want it. Now, my first preference has always been a brotha. If you've ever been with a brotha then you know what I'm talking about. However, if you've never experienced that side of heaven, then you don't know what you're missing. This whole white boy thing took me completely by surprise. I mean, yeah I've seen some fine white boys, and there are a few that I'd consider fuckin', like Tim McGraw and Brad Pitt. Boy, that Tim McGraw could sing to me any day, "She's my kinda rain, like confetti fallin' down on me."

Oh, I got off track; lucky Faith Hill. Anyway, I don't think there's anything wrong with interracial dating. Love is love. I just never thought in a million years that I would seriously date a white man. I have gone out with a few, and we kissed and touched, but I never let it go any further. I just didn't have that feeling. Then Rece spoke to me, and Lord have mercy on my soul 'cause when I looked into those steel gray eyes; I could have died. This white boy literally took my breath away. Fine is an understatement, Rece is delicious.

Rece and I met at the Cracker Barrel near Hickory Hollow Mall. It was around 7:00 a.m. on a Saturday morning. I'd thrown on some sweats, pulled my hair back into a ponytail and put on a little lip gloss. A woman should never leave the house with bare lips. I was reading the newspaper when Rece asked if he could join me. I was a little shocked, but I liked his approach. He was bold. He stepped to me without hesitation. He never wavered or stuttered over his words. He was in control, but he wasn't cocky. It's like he knew what type of woman I was and used that knowledge to approach me. My personality won't allow room for a weak man. Plus, my daddy, my grandfathers and uncles are such strong, intelligent, hardworking men; I can't help but look for those same qualities in a mate. After I told Rece that he could join me, we ate, talked, laughed, exchanged numbers and before I knew it, I was giving up the poo nanny. Let me tell you something, don't believe all of the hype about white men not packing. 'Cause, let me tell you, Rece is a good eight, inching towards nine and he has rhythm. I'm getting wet just thinking about my baby. Whew, enough about Rece. I've got bigger problems and they start with a man by the name of Walter James a.k.a my daddy. My daddy isn't feeling Rece at all. He feels like it's a personal attack against him and it just isn't that way. How can I make him understand that my relationship with Rece just happened? We didn't know that we would meet and fall in love. I don't know what to do. To add to all of my problems, I'm supposed to meet Rece's family. Damn! I wonder what they are going to say about us. He's already warned me about his mother, so I'm preparing myself for the worst.

RECE WILLIAM GALLANTINE

I have always found black women to be beautiful. From the time I entered grade school and saw Michelle Brooks; I knew that I would cross that unspoken line some day. Michelle was the color of caramel candy and had the prettiest braids. I would pull her hair, or put a bug in her chair out of affection. Silly me. She hated me and detested everything that I did to her, but I didn't care. I wanted any ounce of her attention, whether it was bad, good or indifferent. All of it brought me joy. As I got older and started paying closer attention to women; I just found black women more desirable. I love their skin, their hair, and yes, like every man, I am a sucker for their asses.

Although, I've never formally dated a black woman (because my mom would absolutely die); I've longed to just follow my heart. I've never known why people make such a fuss about mixed couples. I mean, you can't help whom you find yourself attracted to or whom you fall in love with. So, when I saw Willow sitting alone; I had to say something. I was smitten. She was dressed in sweats, but the material clung to her body and I could tell that she worked out. She didn't have on any makeup and her skin was flawless. I wanted her, instantly. That's why I didn't hesitate to approach her. Willow is dark chocolate and delectable. Her full lips took my breath away.

However, it wasn't until she looked up that something moved inside of me. I knew in that moment that I had to get to know this woman. Now, the only problem will be convincing my mother to give Willow a chance. Will she be able to see pass Willow's race and see her true beauty? I doubt it. She is so scarred by all of the crap that my dad has put her through that she hates all black people. All because of one black woman that my dad refused to stop seeing. My dad and brother will like Willow. My dad will secretly pat me on the shoulder thinking that he played a part in me pursuing Willow, he will be so wrong. I don't want a relationship that I have to hide. I want the world to know how much I love Willow, but I have a feeling that won't be easy. I can hear my mother screaming at the top of her lungs about how I have ruined the family name by dating a black woman. I'm sure her words will be much harsher. Oh well, she'll get over it, or I won't be around.

"SALAD"

CHAPTER 1

It's Saturday morning and I am starving. I really don't feel like cooking today, so I guess I'll head to the Cracker Barrel for some of their pancakes and turkey sausage. I quickly jump in the shower, throw on a cute sweat suit, pull my hair back and put on some lip gloss. Now that's my number one rule---never go outside without lipstick or lip gloss. Oh, it burns my butt to see a woman with bare lips.

As I am driving down Bell Road, I notice how few people are out at seven o'clock. Am I the only crazy one? I guess so. I pull up to the restaurant, grab me a newspaper and head inside. The aroma of fresh baked biscuits and honey cured ham immediately remind me of my mother's cooking. A robust, redheaded waitress greets me with a warm smile.

"Well, good mornin', darling! How many today?"

"Just one, thank you." I reply, as she grabs a set of utensils and a menu before walking me to a small table near the window.

"Would you like somethin' to drink?"

"A water with lemon and coffee, please. And I already know what I'd like to eat."

"Well, what can I get for you?" she asks.

"I'd like Momma's Pancake Breakfast."

"How ya want yo' eggs?"

"Scrambled."

"What kinda meat?"

"Turkey sausage patties."

"I'll be right back with ya drinks. By the way, my name is Sally and I'll be waitin' on you today."

"Thank you, Miss Sally." I chuckle as I watch her walk away. It looks like Miss Sally has enjoyed quite a bit of Cracker Barrel cooking. Shoot, Miss Sally is probably the reason the food tastes so good. She looks like she can throw down in a kitchen. I flip through my newspaper searching the entertainment section. I want to know who is playing at a few of the jazz clubs this weekend. Miss Sally returns quickly with my water and coffee. I thank her and return to my reading. Just as I am getting ready to turn the page a pleasant voice emerges above me.

"Are you dining alone?" I look up and instantly lose my breath. This fine ass white boy is standing before me. Not only is he standing before me, but I believe he asked me a question. *What was it? Damn!* I get my composure and finally respond.

"Excuse me?" I say, as I examine him a bit closer. *If I must say so, he is an incredible piece of eye cand,y and the fact that he had enough gall to push up on a sistah…well, I guess I can delight him in a little conversation.*

He smiles. Perfect white teeth. "Are you alone? Are eating by yourself?"

"Oh," pausing for a quick moment, "yes."

"I hate eating alone. Is it ok if I share your table?"

"Sure, I could use the company." I say. We both blush as he extends his hand.

"My name is Rece. Rece Gallantine." His hands are strong…a little rough, but in a nice way. He probably does some type of manual labor.

"I'm Willow."

"Mmmm, Willow. That's a beautiful name. It suits you perfectly." *I know this white boy ain't coming on like this. I must say, I like his confidence.*

"Thank you, Mr. Gallantine. You sure are forward."

"No, not really. I'm actually quite reserved, but when I saw you walk in I had to say something. And since you appeared to be alone, I couldn't let an opportunity like this slip by." Throwing up his hands, "Can you really blame me? My God, you're beautiful!" He chuckles.

"Well, since you put it like that…no, I can't." We both laugh.

Miss Sally returns with two plates and smiles. "I see that ya switched places on me, sir."

"Yes, ma'am."

"Good, it's not good to eat alone." She says as she places our plates on the table. We thank her and she tells us to just yell if we want anything else. Rece and I talk as if we've been friends forever. He's easy to talk to and even has a good sense of humor. I must admit that I am a bit surprised that I let him join me, but I'm glad that I did.

"So, Willow, is it possible to see you, again? I mean, may I take you out on a real date?" He rubs his hands together as if he's nervous. I laugh on the inside. *Should I make him sweat? Nah, I think I'd enjoy myself.*

"What's a real date?"

"You know, where I pick you up and take you some place special."

"Like the Cracker Barrel?" I ask, as we both laugh.

"Well, let me put this way. We can go wherever you'd like." He leans back and flashes that beautiful smile, again.

"Okay, sure. You've got my attention. Now let's see if you can keep it!"

"I'll give it my best shot," he says while licking his lips. He takes a bite of his eggs.

Damn! Damn! Damn! Lord help me. Keep me near the cross 'cause a sista is getting turned on. I don't know where the time has gone, but Miss Sally is back with our checks.

"Well, ya'll look like ya havin' so much fun, I didn't want to botha' ya," Miss Sally says while placing both of our checks on the table. Rece grabs both checks.

"Rece?" I say.

"Yes, Willow."

"Thank you, darling, but I can handle my check." I reach out to take my check from him and he just pulls them closer to his chest.

"No, thank you. You have absolutely made my morning…I insist." Rece takes care of the tab and we walk outside and exchange numbers. We agree that we will touch base during the week. I thank him again for breakfast and we part ways.

Wow! Did I just agree to go on a date with Rece? Am I out of my mind? I mean, I've done the casual white boy thing, but something actually moved inside of me today. Something I haven't felt in a very long time. Not since Jordan have I felt this feeling of excitement. Shoot, this can't be happening. Am I ready to date? Can I muster up the courage to open myself up again? I gotta call my girl, Journey. As I'm reaching for my cell phone, it starts to ring.

"Hello."

"Thanks again for breakfast."

"You're more than welcome." *Why am I smiling like I've won the lottery? Stop it Willow!*

"Willow, I know that we said we'd touch base during the week, but if you don't have any plans this evening, maybe we can meet for drinks?"

"That will work." *What the hell did I just say? Mouth shut up!* "Do you know where Sambuca is located?"

"Yes, I do." He replies.

"How about I meet you there around eight?" *Mouth you are still running…shut up. I mean it!*

"That's perfect. I look forward to seeing you."

"Bye, Rece."

"Bye, Willow."

Willow, Willow, Willow! Are you crazy? He's white! I know that. Why can't I go on a date with nice guy regardless of his race? Whatever! You better not bring a white boy home to meet your dad. All hell will break loose. Whatever, I'm grown. I quickly dial Journey's number.

CHAPTER 2

Journey Jones. Journey and I have been best friends since high school. We both attended Martin Luther King, Jr. Magnet School and were both bookworms. We actually met while in the library. We started laughing out loud at the same time, looked up at each other and noticed that we were reading the same book, *Ugly Ways* by Tina McElroy Ansa. We've been thick as thieves ever since. Journey and I are like night and day. I'm relatively calm, she's emotional. She says what's on her mind, I ponder long and hard before saying anything. Unless it's involving someone I truly care about, then I can be explosive. If you hurt Journey, it shows all over her face. If you hurt me, you'd never know. I keep the perfect poker face. We tend to balance each other out. She and I are both only children and as our parents would say, "spoiled rotten". Oh well, we wouldn't change a thing, we're sisters. Journey has been on me lately about dating again. She has even set me up on some blind dates, but I just wasn't interested. Plus, it's been awkward since her boyfriend Devin is best friends with my ex. So, it's a little complicated.

I was so distraught after Jordan and I broke up that I really didn't want the drama of a new relationship, but Journey helped me to see that my life had to continue with or without Jordan. She was my calm during the storm. For three years she dealt with my ups and downs. So, I think she'll be pleased about me going out on a date, but I'll wait to tell her that he's white.

"Hello."

"Hey, Journey! What's up?"

"Ah, nothing. Just getting dressed. What are you up to?" She asks, sounding devilish.

I pause for a moment and then say, "Nothing much, and maybe a little bit of something."

We both laugh.

"Willow, what have you gotten into?"

"Who me?" I sigh.

"Yes, you. You do know that I know you."

"Well, I met a guy today."

"Thank you, Jesus! Finally! Okay, give me the dirt. Who is he? Where is he from?" She spurts out quicker than a speed talker.

"Whoa, slow down, sweetie." I reply.

I hear Journey take a deep breath and then she says, "Okay, I'm listening…oooh lord, Willow has met a man."

"Keep playing and I won't tell you anything!" I snap jokingly.

"Okay, okay."

"Well, I went to Cracker Barrel this morning for breakfast and this guy sees me sitting alone and asks if he could join me and I said yes."

"Wow, for you to say yes, he has got to have some major flavor."

"Girrrrrl, fine is an understatement," I giggle.

"Oh, oh. Could this be a love connection?" Journey inquires.

"Hold on, Journey. I just met him. However, we are meeting for drinks tonight."

"Mmmmmm, what's his name?" She asks coyly.

"His name is Rece. Rece Gallantine."

"Girl, he sounds like royalty."

We both crack up laughing.

"Journey, you are crazy."

"Naw, I'm just happy to see my girl back in the game. What are you wearing on your date?"

"I don't know. I may run by Coco's and pick up a really cute outfit."

"Alright, I gotta run. Devin and I are going to pick out a gift for his mom's birthday. Call me after your date, okay?"

"Okay."

"Promise?" Journey asks.

"I promise."

"Love you."

"I love you too, Journey. Bye."

I hang up and smile. Journey can always make me laugh. And she's right, it does feel good to be going out again. I do believe that I'm excited. Wow! This is too much.

CHAPTER 3

I pull up in front of my house and just sit in my truck for a moment. I need a minute to catch my breath. I am smitten…blown away. Did I not just meet the most beautiful woman in the world? Damn! Willow, Willow, Willow. Man, this is unreal. I haven't been to Cracker Barrel in over a year, but I was craving their pancakes and turkey sausage. Evidently, so was Willow. *Okay, Rece, get yourself together, you have a date tonight.*

First, let me go in the house and order some flowers for Willow. I wonder what kind she likes? Maybe a nice fall arrangement? As I'm stepping inside my front door I hear my telephone ring; but I decide to let my answering machine pick up. I know it's my mom.

"Rece, darling, it's your mother. Call me when you get in. I am having a dinner party on Friday and guess who's coming? Yes, I have invited Heather and her parents! She is such a lovely girl Rece, and she comes from such a lovely family. Don't disappoint your mother. This Friday, six o'clock sharp. I love you."

My goodness! When will my mother stop? She has been trying for years to set me up with "*somebody's daughter*" and it never works. She keeps reminding me that she wants to be able to enjoy her grandchildren and then she'll throw in a sly remark like, "That is, whenever I have grandchildren!" Man, it drives me crazy. I can understand wanting your son to be married, but I don't want to marry someone just because they come from a wealthy family. I want to be in love. I want the woman of my dreams to be my best friend. I want to melt when I see her. Not pretend just to keep wealth and influence in the family. My mother is superficial that way.

Don't get me wrong, I love my mother, but there are some things about her that I simply don't care for. She's been nagging me lately for not coming around the house often enough. Well, if she would stop this whole matchmaking deal; I would come around more. I'm sorry, but I am choosing my own wife, and the family had better get that in their heads. Especially my mom. Maybe I should show up with Willow. Boy, that would be a mess. I'll wait and see how this new friendship blossoms before exposing her to the Gallantine Family.

CHAPTER 4

Whew! I'm a little tired after running ten miles. Saturday mornings are dedicated to my long runs. You would think that I would be used to running this distance after ten years, but every now and again I feel beat afterwards. I think it was the pancakes. Normally, I would eat afterwards, but this morning I couldn't resist. Or, maybe I just wasn't focused on running? Maybe, I couldn't get Rece out of my head? *Probably, the latter!* I mean yes, he is good looking, but to my surprise he was also very personable and had a great sense of humor. I love a man that can make me laugh.

Let me not get ahead of myself. I'll get a better feel for Mr. Gallantine tonight. Until then, I think I'll take a long, hot bath and just pamper me for a moment. Before I do any of that, I better call my mom before she starts blowing up my phone.

"James' residence," She says in a most articulate tone.

"Hi, Mama." I reply.

"Hello, baby, how's my sweetheart?"

"I'm good, Mama. What are you up to?"

"Oh, I am sitting here by the fireplace enjoying a cup of coffee and reading the new *O Magazine*."

"Mmmm, that sounds good. Where's Daddy?"

She chuckles. "Now you know where your father is. At the golf course…where else?"

"I should have known. He should own the course by now, huh?" We both laugh.

"What are you doing, baby? I thought I was going to see you today."

"Well, I thought about coming over tonight but," I pause for moment to gather my thoughts before speaking, "I have a date."

Silence. "You have a what?" She asks in total shock.

"A date, Mama. You do know that I am not immune to dating."

"Really?" She replies sarcastically. "You wouldn't know that by the way you have been moping around here for three years."

"Mama, I haven't been moping, I've just been taking some time out for me. Trying to figure out who I really am, that's all."

"Okay, you can call it what you want, but I know when my baby is moping. Don't forget, I birthed you into this world and I know when you are moping."

"Mama, stop! You're a mess." I laugh.

"Well, baby, I'm glad that you're going on a date. Who is this lucky gentleman?"

"His name is Rece Gallantine and I met him this morning while having breakfast."

"Rece, huh?" She responds inquisitively. "Okay, well I hope that you have a good time and give me the scoop at dinner tomorrow night."

"I will. Oh, tell Daddy hello for me."

"Okay." Mom takes a slight pause. "Baby?"

"Yes."

"Remember to be open to the possibility of falling in love again, okay?"

"I will, Mama."

"I love you."

"I love you, too."

As I lay my phone on the cradle, I smile. I really love my mom even though she can be a mess. Now, Mrs. James is the ultimate diva. You will never see her break a sweat or lose her composure, but she's like a tiger if you try to hurt her cub. My mom is very direct, and sometimes it hurts to hear some of the things that she says. But, she has always been honest with me about any and everything, so I trust her beyond words. She and my dad were really worried about me after Jordan and I broke up.

They really loved Jordan, but they saw early on that Jordan was not ready to settle down. They would always say that he was nice and smart, but really lacked focus when it came to his goals. They never believed that he would be their son-in-law. However, you'd never know it, because they treated him with such love and care. It wasn't until that last blowup when my dad made a visit to Jordan's home, and told him that if he was not going to honor me in every way… to simply leave me alone. He also told him that if he hurt me again; his next visit would not include talking. Needless to say, we broke up the very next day. I had never seen my dad so angry. I guess he had just seen enough of me crying and felt as if he needed to intervene. In hindsight, I'm glad that he did, because the reality was that Jordan was not ready for real commitment.

I hurt for months. It felt as if my insides had been ripped out. I couldn't eat or sleep, but eventually things got better. One day of no crying turned into two days of no crying, which turned into a month of no crying. Before I knew it, I simply didn't cry anymore. The hurt was gone. Yes, it took a while, but when you truly love someone that love does not stop overnight, I don't care what anyone says.

Anyway, that chapter of my life is closed and I am looking forward to better days. Jordan is a good person, just not good for me. Oh well, you live and you learn.

CHAPTER 5

It's about eight o'clock when I pull up to Sambuca and valet my car. This area right off of 12th Avenue is becoming quite the buzz in Nashville. A lot of hip restaurants and clubs are attracting quite a few singles. I immediately notice Rece standing out front. My goodness, I thought that he was breathtaking in casual clothes, but he cleans up mighty well. He smiles when he realizes that it's me. I can tell that I'm taking his breath away slowly. I am looking rather hot if I must say so. I didn't want to give him a heart attack, just a murmur. That's why I settled on this fitted, black, cold shoulder dress that hits right at mid-thigh.

As I approach Rece, I can feel myself getting butterflies. *Willow, it's just a date. Come on now, chill!*

"Hello, Rece."

He reaches for both of my hands and pulls me close to him. "Hello, Willow," he says before kissing me on my cheek. *Damn! Damn! He smells good. Shit! Shit!*

"You look beautiful."

"Thank you. You aren't too shabby yourself." I reply.

"I try," he says.

We both laugh.

While still holding one of my hands, Rece leads me into the restaurant to an intimate table. I immediately notice the beautiful bouquet of flowers. Rece pulls out my chair and hands me the bouquet.

"These are for you."

Blushing, I respond, "Thank you, Rece, I love them."

"You're welcome. Now, what would you like to drink?"

"Mmmm, how about a glass of Merlot."

"Merlot it is." Rece motions for the waitress and orders us a bottle of Leonetti.

While we're waiting for our drinks, we enjoy the sounds of the live jazz band that's playing.

"Willow, thanks for joining me."

"No problem, but I have to admit something."

"What's that?" He asks as he leans back in his chair.

"I started to say no."

"Why? Did I do something wrong?"

"No, it's not that. It's just that I haven't really dated since my last relationship, and I just got bummed out on the whole dating scene."

"Well, I can surely understand that. I haven't had much luck either."

With a bit of curiosity I say, "Come on, an attractive man as yourself surely doesn't have any problems getting women."

"I'm flattered, but I could easily say the same thing about you. It's rough being a single man."

"Really? How so?"

"Well, if it's not my mom trying to fix me up so that she can have grandchildren, it's my family and friends. Everyone wants me to settle down. They just don't understand. I will know when I've found true love."

"You think so?"

"Yeah, I do." He smiles.

"Now don't get me wrong, I do date. However, I haven't come across the one that stops me in my tracks…at least not until I saw you."

"Wow, you're good." I say while laughing.

"No, seriously, Willow." He stares intently into my eyes. "Sure, I could have just spoke and went about my business, but something told me to approach you. And you know what? I'm glad that I did."

"Me, too. You seem like a nice guy. Forgive me for being so nonchalant. It's not fair to you."

"No problem."

The waitress returns with our bottle of wine. Rece takes a sip and nods at the waitress. She pours our wine and leaves.

"Shall we toast?" Rece asks.

"Sure. What would you like to toast to?" I ask.

"How about to new friendships?"

"That will work."

We toast.

Rece moves his chair around the table so that he can be closer to me.

"Do you mind?"

"No, it's ok." *I can't believe I said that.*

"Good."

Rece grabs my hand and gently holds it through several songs. I don't flinch or pull away. His hand feels good next to mine. *Am I really letting him hold my hand? Girl, you are showing out and losing your mind. First, you had to say yes and now you're holding his hand! This is too much, but I haven't enjoyed myself like this in a long time. Oh well…*

Chapter 6

Rece and I finally left Sambuca around midnight. I had a really nice time. He is such a gentleman and he makes me laugh. I had better call Journey before she has a fit.

"Hello."

"Hey girl, it's me."

"Hi, Willow. I take it that you are back from your hot date?" She chuckles.

"Yes, I am back and I had a great time!"

"Well, that's good. I was praying that this would be a successful date, cuz I couldn't deal with another disaster date."

"You? I don't think I can take another goof ball."

"So, do you think you'll see Rece, again?" Journey asks.

"I think so. I mean, what could it hurt?"

"That's my girl! Get back in the game!"

We both laugh.

"You are a mess, Journey."

"No, seriously. I'm just glad that you had a date and you had a good time."

"I know. It's been a while, but I am now on a new chapter." I reply.

"Okay, tell me more about this Rece fella'. What does he look like? Did you kiss him?"

Laughing. "No, I did not kiss him. He was a complete gentleman and uh..."

"Uh, what?" With a little pep in her voice.

"Okay, Journey, I won't be able to keep this from you much longer so I am just going to spit it out."

"What? Now you have me nervous."

"Rece is white." I say calmly.

"He's what?" Totally surprised.

"You heard me, he's white."

"Girl, get the fuck outta here! You did not go out with a white boy!" She's laughing.

"Yes, I did, and I really enjoyed myself."

"He has got to be Brad Pitt fine for you to give him any kind of action."

I laugh and say, "That he is. I can't wait for you guys to meet. That is if he stays on point."

"Well, I am still in shock. Oh my, what are your parents going to say?"

"Don't go there. I haven't gotten that far yet. Let's just see what happens."

"Well, you're my girl and I just want to see you happy and loved. If the person who provides this happens to be white, oh well." She blurts, matter-of-factly.

"Journey, don't get me wrong. I was hesitant to go out with Rece because of the whole white thing, but then I thought that was a poor excuse to turn someone down. Shoot, a nice guy is a nice guy."

"You're right. So, when is the next date?"

"We're supposed to get together next weekend."

"Okay. Keep me posted and just remember that love knows no color."

"I know, but I am still a little scared."

"Willow?"

"Yes, Journey?"

"Let it flow. Isn't that what Toni Braxton says?"

"Yeah, you're right."

"I'll talk to you later."

"Goodnight, Journey."

"Goodnight, Willow."

I sit in my chaise lounge and throw my chenille throw over my feet. Wow, this evening actually turned out nice. I lay my head back and just play back the events of the day. I find myself smiling at the thought of seeing Rece again. *I believe that I'd like that very much, very much indeed.*

CHAPTER 7

It's early Sunday morning and I decide to fix a pot of coffee. I'm a little exhausted because I didn't get any rest last night. Images of Willow occupied every ounce of my brain. I had a really good time with her. I wanted to call her last night and talk some more, but I didn't want it to appear as if I was coming on too strong. I need to take my time with this one.

I am surprised at how comfortable I felt around her. What's even more amazing is that she got all of my jokes. I like that. It also felt good holding her hand. I needed to touch some part of her. When she got out of her car and I saw her in that black dress, I just about died. Willow is just fine. There is no other way to describe her. I wonder if she is up this early in the morning? Nah, I'll just wait and call her later on today.

I grab my morning paper from the front porch and then head back into my kitchen to pour a cup of fresh java. Sliding onto my barstool, I immediately start flipping through the paper trying to find the sports section. My phone rings and I look at the caller ID, it's my mom.

"Hi, Mom."

"Hello, darling. How's my handsome son doing this morning?" She asks, in her usual cheery tone.

"I'm fine, mom. How are you?"

"Fantastic! I just finished my morning walk, and your dad and I are about to have breakfast."

"Tell Dad hello for me."

"I will. Did you get my message yesterday?" She asks with a bit of molasses in her tone.

"Yes."

"And?"

"And what?"

"And, are you coming?"

"Mom, listen."

"Okay, am I in trouble?"

I pause for a moment. "No, Mom, you are not in trouble, but we need to talk."

"I'm listening." She says, like a child that's about to be punished.

"Okay. I'll come to dinner on Friday, but this is the absolute last time that I want you trying to set me up with someone."

"But."

"But nothing, Mom. This is it! I am fully capable of finding a woman on my own!" I snap.

"Well darling, you haven't brought anyone home in years and Heather is such good stock."

"There you go. I don't care about Heather's stock, Mom. I need to be interested. I need to feel something."

"Oh baby, just give it some time."

"No, this is the last time and I am quite serious."

"Well, I am just trying to help and I would at least like to see some grandchildren before I'm old and senile."

I laugh out loud. "Mom, I am not going down this road with you, again. Stop trying to set me up and things will be fine."

She sighs. "At the rate you're going, you're going to miss out on all of the good girls in Nashville."

"Really?" I ask.

"Yes, really." She replies.

"As a matter-of-fact, I had a date last night with a lovely woman."

"What?" She exclaims. "Who is she? Who are her people?"

"None of your business." I say softly, which I know will drive her crazy.

"Rece!"

"Goodbye, Mom. I'll see you on Friday, and remember no more setups. Love you."

"Rece!"

"Bye, Mom." I hang up before she gets her next sentence out. She immediately calls back, but this time I let my voice mail pick up.

My mother. You gotta love her. She means well, but she drives me crazy trying to set me up with every affluent, single woman she comes across. First, there was Ginger Hellwell, daughter of Senator Hellwell. Then Becky Stallworth, daughter of Judge Stallworth. Then Samantha Winston, daughter of Congressman Winston. Now, it's Heather Goldstein, daughter of Attorney Donald Goldstein. Don't get me wrong, all of these women have been nice and very attractive, but beyond that…nothing. They were all just nice eye candy, no substance. Let's take Heather for instance. She can tell you all about the latest fashions from Paris, but she can't discuss any social issue. She has been taught to focus all of her energy on being beautiful and submissive. It is a huge turn off for me. I grew up around that shit and I don't plan on living like my parents. I want someone who wants me for me, period. Not someone who just wants to be a part of the social privileged. Plus, Heather has already had enough plastic surgery to last a lifetime. I do not want to wake up every morning to a Joan Rivers look-alike. I want someone who is naturally beautiful, and not because of tons of plastic surgery.

I also want someone that is willing to work and contribute to the household. Not someone who believes that just because she is attractive, and sucks my dick every now and again, that she shouldn't have to work or that I should feel honored to take care of her. No way. The fact that my future wife wouldn't have to work a day in her life is a huge plus, but I want to know that she at least desires to assist me. That desire alone will make me want to take care of her. It will make me say, "Honey, you can do whatever you like. I got this!"

Maybe I'll just cancel and not go. I'm sure that would *not* go over well with my mom. But who cares at this point? I'll have to give it some more thought. Thank goodness I have a week.

Let me focus on something else. *Ah, Willow…now that's a beautiful thought.*

CHAPTER 8

I open the door to my parent's home and the smell of good southern cooking overpowers my nostrils. I can already taste the candied yams. Mmmm. As I am laying my things down, my mom yells from the kitchen.

"Willow, is that you, baby?"

"Yes, Mama, it's me."

I walk into the kitchen and Mama is pulling a ham out of the oven. I walk over and kiss her on the cheek.

"Hi, Mama."

"Hi, baby. Are you just getting out of church?"

"Yes. The service went a little long today, because we had that guest speaker from Memphis."

"Oh, that's right. Was he any good?" Mom inquires.

"Actually, he was."

"That's good. Your dad and I decided to stay home today. We were just tired after being at the revival all week long." She says, while handing me the silverware to place on the table.

"I can understand that. By the way, where is Daddy?"

"He's out back in his garden."

I open the French doors that lead to the backyard, "Hi, Daddy!" I yell.

Dad is on his hands and knees. He is meticulous about his vegetable garden. He has never trusted all of the pesticides used on food, so he plants his own stuff. It's nothing like fresh collards straight from the garden.

He looks up and smiles.

"Hey, baby girl. Tell your mom that I'll be in shortly."

"Okay." I reply and close the doors. I continue setting the table when Mama walks towards me and says in a slick tone, "Okay, I'm waiting Little Miss. I'm waiting."

Knowing full well what she is speaking about, I choose to play naïve. "What?"

"Girl, don't play with me. You know what. Tell me about your hot date."

"Oh, that." I say coyly.

"Yes, that." She snaps. "Come on, before your dad gets in here."

We both start laughing because she always wants to know stuff before Dad.

"Well, he's quite charming, and I had a very nice time with him. He didn't try too hard or overdo it. He was very relaxed and a complete gentleman." I find myself smiling.

"That's nice. What does he do for a living?" She asks, while placing the rolls on the table.

"He didn't really talk about what he does, but from the conversation I gather it's something with construction."

"Does he go to church?"

"I don't know"

"Umph!" She crosses her eyes at me.

"Did he attend college?"

"Yes, Vanderbilt."

"Ever been married?"

"No."

"Any children?"

"No."

"Socially conscience?"

"Seems to be?"

"Democrat or Republican?

"Don't know?"

"Alright, that's enough for now. I'm just glad that you had a nice time. You're too smart and beautiful to not have an active social life." She walks around the table and hugs me. "I love you."

"I love you, too, Mama."

Just then my dad walks in. I give him a big hug and kiss, and he walks towards the stove and lifts one of the lids. "I'm hungry, woman." He kids with my mama.

"Well, wash up, and then you can eat." He wraps his arms around her and nibbles at her ear. "I'll eat you if you don't watch it." She giggles.

"Oh, Walter, stop that." She says, while gently breaking away from him. I see him tap her on the behind before heading off to the bathroom. My parents. They crack me up. If you were to ever meet them, you would think that they had just gotten married. I mean, they still light up when they see each other. *Wow! I want that type of love someday.*

Daddy returns and we all sit down as he leads us in prayer. For as long as I can remember, we've always had a big Sunday dinner. It's our special time together and Mama always cooks our favorite foods. Plus there is always enough left over for me to have meals for a whole week.

"Well, baby girl, your mom tells me that you had a date. Is that true?" He asks while reaching for the collards.

"Yes, Daddy, it's true."

"There is a God!" Dad teases.

"Oh, you got jokes now, huh?"

We all burst into laughter.

"No, I'm just happy that you're dating, again. I won't drill you." He says, while looking over at my mama who smiles, and then lowers her eyes to avoid looking at him. "Because I am sure that your mom took care of that." He says, sarcastically.

"Well, a mother has to know who is taking her daughter out." She sighs.

"Yeah, yeah. All you really need to know is whether or not Willow had a good time." He responds, with a slick grin.

"And that I did." I interject. "Rece seems to be a nice guy."

"Okay then, I'll just stay tuned." He says.

We eat our fabulous meal and discuss everything from news to politics, to sports and of course the latest family drama. My cousin Sharday is pregnant, again. This is baby number four and baby daddy number four. Damn, can't she keep her legs closed? Now, she needs her tubes tied like yesterday. It's just down right pitiful. But, as always, my parents will help her out and make sure that she has everything that she needs. My mom always says that you should never turn your back on family, and that we all require grace. Her favorite question: "Willow, what if God didn't grant you grace? Where would you be?" I hate when she asks me that. I know that she's right, but four babies, by four different men, is a hot ass mess. No matter how you slice it and that's that.

CHAPTER 9

I get home around seven and quickly put the food Mama packed for me away. Since I don't have any clients tomorrow, I think that I'll just take it easy tonight. That's one of the luxuries of being self-employed. I set my own schedule. It's absolutely wonderful. I'm a life coach. You heard me right. I basically get paid for teaching people how to improve their lives. Pretty amazing.

It actually started as a fluke. After graduating from Fisk University with a master's degree in Psychology, I worked as a guidance counselor at McGavock High School for six years. During that time, I started conducting free self-enhancement seminars for women.

The seminars became so popular that I found myself working nearly every weekend. One day, after a seminar, a woman approached me and asked how much I charged for one-on-one sessions. Well, I had never charged for my services. These seminars were a part of me giving back to my community. Anyway, she gave me her number and I called her the following week. We agreed on an hourly rate and the rest is history. She told several of her friends, and the next thing I knew, I had over fifty clients. I love what I do, but more than that, I love the results. I have a way of pulling out the best in people. It's definitely a gift from God. I just wonder why it hasn't worked with my love life. Who knows?

My phone rings. It's Rece. I find myself blushing.

"Hello."

"Yes, may I speak to Willow, please?"

"Well, it depends." I say teasingly.

"On what?" He asks with a sweet, inquisitive tone.

"How bad do you want to speak to Willow?"

"Desperately, I've been thinking about her all day."

"Mmmm, since you put it that way, hello, Rece."

He laughs. "Hi, Willow. How are you?"

"Wonderful. And yourself?"

"I'm good. Did I catch you at a bad time?"

"No, I was just relaxing. I had dinner with my parents earlier and now I'm just taking it easy. How was your day?

"Actually it was nice. I took care of some much needed things around the house, caught up on some reading and watched a few basketball games."

"Sounds good to me."

"Believe me, I could think of a million things that I would have rather been doing."

"Like what?"

"Like seeing you."

I chuckle. "Surely you have better things to do?"

"I can't think of one."

I giggle at his response.

"Willow?"

"Yes, Rece."

"Stop me if I am being too forward. Okay?"

"Okay." I brace myself because I really don't know what is about to come out of Rece's mouth.

I can hear him taking in a deep breath. "Do I have to wait until the end of the week to see you, or can I see you tonight?"

I let out a small sigh. "You had me going there for a moment, I thought it was something bad."

He laughs. "Oh, I'm sorry. I just didn't want to come across too pushy."

"I would like to see you, again, Rece." *Shit, did that just pop out of my mouth? Girl, you are just jumping into this dating thing full throttle!*

"Would you like to meet somewhere?" He quickly asks.

"No, why don't you come over to my place around eight or so." *No I didn't! No I did not just tell that man that he could come over to my house. Lord, Jesus help me. Help me now!*

"That sounds good. I'll bring the wine."

I can sense him smiling.

I give Rece directions to my home and quickly remove my Sunday attire. *Wow! I actually invited Rece to my house? Am I losing my mind? Shoot, I don't know! Oooh, I'm scared, nervous and excited, all at once. I'm a mess, but I like it!*

CHAPTER 10

I decide to put on a fitted cami with matching yoga pants. After lighting a few chamomile candles, I reach for the remote and turn on the satellite radio to a nice jazz station. I pull together a small cheese, fruit and cracker tray, since Rece is bringing the wine. Maybe I'll even turn on the fireplace, just for the ambiance. I'm a true romantic. The security guard calls and informs me that my guest has arrived. A few minutes later, my doorbell rings and I immediately feel the butterflies inside of my stomach going crazy. *Calm down, Willow.* I count to ten, look through my peep hole and open the door. *Lord, this man is fine!*

I welcome Rece into my home. He looks good. He's wearing a pair of jeans, a melon colored pullover and a nice pair of Gucci slip-ons. He hands me a bottle of wine and gently kisses me near the corner of my mouth. We're both blushing.

"Thanks for the wine. Have a seat and I'll grab some glasses." As I'm walking into the kitchen, Rece comments on my home.

"Willow, you have a beautiful place. It looks like you."

"Really?" I ask.

"Yes, it's beautifully decorated, yet inviting. Not to mention the detail of your columns and molding. Your builder did a good job."

"Oh, I forgot that you're into construction." I say, while handing Rece the wine and the wine opener. I sit the glasses down in front of him. He's looking around the room and taking in every detail.

"Yes, and so the little things catch my eye." He points to my floors. "Like these floors, I know that these are Rehmeyer floors." Rece kneels down and runs his hands across the wood. "I use Rehmeyer a lot in my custom homes."

"Wow! I guess you know your stuff. I'm impressed."

"I know, it's a little weird."

"No, actually, it's impressive. So, you build houses for living?"

"Yeah." He says, while pouring the wine.

"Do you love what you do?"

"I do, I can't imagine doing anything else. I guess it's in my blood." Rece sits on the sofa, and I plop down on the other side.

"Well, that's good. I think everyone should enjoy their work." I say, while grabbing the glass of wine that Rece is handing me.

We tap glasses.

"It's good to see you." He pauses before flashing that dazzling smile. "Again."

"Likewise."

We can't contain our smiles. It's like we're teenagers.

Rece and I talk for hours. The time just seemed to sail by. I found out that he's a Dallas Cowboys fan, so he gets twenty extra points for that alone. We finish the bottle of wine and Rece stands up and takes a few steps towards me. He grabs my hands and lifts me from the sofa. He runs his fingers through my hair, gently grabs my face and gives me the most delectable kiss ever. It is soft and sweet. I suddenly feel warm and I let my body melt against his. He pulls me closer and parts my lips with his tongue. His mouth is on fire and I'm loving it. He moans and then pulls away. I think we both are a little embarrassed.

"I'd better get going." He whispers.

"Okay, thanks for coming by." I whisper in return.

"No", pausing for a moment to look into my eyes, "thank you." He says before kissing me, again.

"Good night, Willow."

"Good night, Rece."

I close the door and try to catch my breath. Just as I'm about to blow out all of the candles, my phone rings.

"Hello."

"Willow?"

"Yes."

"Soon?"

"Yes, really soon."

"Sleep well."

"You, too."

CHAPTER 11

It's the crack of dawn as I am pulling in front of our corporate office. I see my dad pulling up beside me. He amazes me. After working for over thirty years, he still comes to the office every day. At first, it used to bother me because I thought he didn't trust my brother and me to run the business. However, I found out that he just couldn't retire and golf like most men. He has to have his fingers in or on something. So, every day he stops by the office, has a cup of coffee, looks over some paper work, asks a few questions and then he leaves. I am positive that it's his way of keeping tabs on us, but I don't mind. He spent years building this company and he just can't remove himself that easily. We aren't the number one builder in Tennessee by accident. Dad sacrificed his heart and soul for WG Enterprises and just expects the same from his boys. My younger brother Bronson runs the office and I spend most of my time locating investment property and building new communities.

For the past five years WG Enterprises has focused on affordable housing. I believe that everyone deserves a home of their own. It's the American dream. So, WG pays all closing costs for first-time home buyers that purchase with us. We also give them an extra thousand dollars to help with household purchases. It's our way of giving back. Of course, my passion is building custom homes. I haven't built my dream home yet, but hopefully that will happen soon. Or, whenever I find Mrs. Right.

I grab my briefcase and step out of my truck. Dad is walking towards me. He walks a little slower since having knee surgery, but he's still in excellent shape.

"Good morning, son."

"Hi, Dad. How are you?"

We embrace.

"Oh, I'm good, son. Where's Bronson?" He asks while looking around the parking lot for Bronson's truck.

"Remember? He and Mindy are having their home visit with the adoption agency today."

"Oh, that's right. I hope everything goes well. Those two deserve a baby of their own."

"Yeah, they do."

My brother and his wife have been trying, with no luck, for four years to get pregnant. It has been very trying for the both of them. Like most couples, they just assumed that they would be able to have children, but it just never happened. Doctors couldn't find anything wrong with either of them. So, this year they decided that they had enough of doctors, pills and injections, and were going to adopt. This process has been long, but they know that it is well worth it. I can't wait to be an uncle. Uncle Rece. That has a nice ring to it.

Dad and I walk into the office and are greeted immediately by Jennifer, our receptionist. Jennifer is godsent. She's been with the company a little over twenty years, and has never missed a day. I can't imagine WG Enterprises without her.

"Good morning, Mr. Gallantine." She says, while handing Dad his mail.

"Good morning, Jen." He replies.

"Hi, Rece."

"Good morning, Jen." I say, as I walk towards my office. I always smile at how Jen acknowledges us. Dad is always "Mr." and Bronson and I are just "Bronson"and "Rece". Jen says that we aren't old enough to be called "Mr."; I guess not in her eyes. She follows us into my office, places my mail on the desk, and pours my dad and I each a cup of coffee. Jen asks if we need anything else, and then leaves.

"Son, how are things going?" Dad asks, while getting himself comfortable in the leather arm chair.

"Things are good, Dad."

"I drove by the new subdivision in East Nashville. It looks good. Actually, it looks like my work."

We both chuckle. My dad is far from modest.

"Well, you did teach me everything that I know."

"Yeah, I know that. But, I like how you haven't forgotten about the small details that make a home appealing."

"I'll never forget that Dad." I take a sip of coffee and lean back into my chair.

"Good. Now, let's talk." Dad places his coffee cup on my desk and leans forward.

"What is it?" I ask, even though I already know that it is about mom.

"Your mother and this goddamn dinner party!" He runs his fingers through his hair. "Man, she just won't stop!" He says.

"I know. We talked the other day and I told her that this is the last matchmaking escapade that I am attending. Period." I take a sip of my coffee.

"She means well, son, but she just goes too far sometimes. I told her that this has to stop and that you are more than capable of finding your own woman."

"Thank goodness. At least you understand." I sigh.

"I do, son, and your mom has promised me that this is it." He pauses for a moment and then smiles. "Well, let's just say that I made her promise."

"Whatever works." I reply, as we laugh in unison.

"Now, tell me about this date you had."

"She's nice, Dad. I really enjoyed myself." I smile at the thought of Willow.

"Is this one a keeper?"

"I don't know yet, but I'm really feeling her."

"You should bring her by the house." He says, while enjoying his fresh brew.

"We'll see." I say, as I start opening my mail.

"Just hurry up. Your mom is driving me crazy about grandkids." Dad grabs his coffee mug and walks towards the door.

"Well, look at it this way. If Bronson and Mindy's adoption goes through, Mom will get her wish."

"Yeah, yeah. But you know your mom. She'll love the baby, but sooner or later she'll make a comment about it not being blood."

"Dad!" I exclaim, not out of anger, but of shock that he actually said it.

"Hey, I love your mom, but I don't always like her."

"Believe me, I understand."

"Bye, son. See you on Friday." He chuckles.

"Bye, Dad." He walks out of my office and I lean back in my seat. I can't help but laugh to myself. He really knows his wife. I see that she's getting on his nerves, too. Ahhh, family.

CHAPTER 12

Wow! I'm really digging Rece. I mean, I can't believe that I like him. It shouldn't be that big of a deal. Or should it? He's a man. I'm a woman. We're attracted to each other. We enjoy each other's company. So, what's the problem? He's white for one and I'm black. Well, Willow that's never going to change. So, you might as well get over it. What's so strange is that when I am with Rece, his color is not an issue. He's just a man. I'm not saying that I don't notice his skin color. It's just that the more I talk to Rece, the more his skin color just fades to the back and I am drawn to who he is as a person. And what I see so far seems to be quite genuine. I mean, he listens when I talk and he pays attention to details. For instance, the other night I happened to mention that I like a good Riesling. What does he do? When he came over he had a nice German Riesling. Small, but important. He was paying attention. Oh, and let me not forget that he is a great kisser and he knows how to hold me. A sistah has got to give him some points for that. Mr. Gallantine is starting off on a good note. Will he withstand the test of time? Or will he fall by the wayside? Only time will tell. I just hope that he doesn't have a small penis, because that would soooo mess up everything. Call me selfish, but I want it all. And for all of you out there saying that size doesn't matter…bullshit! And that's real talk. I crack myself up.

CHAPTER 13

Friday seemed to get here quicker than usual. Maybe it's because I have been dreading this day all week. I really don't feel like sitting through a boring dinner just to please my mother, but I guess my feelings really don't matter. I would much rather be spending my time with Willow. We've spoken every day this week and each day the conversation gets better. She is so refreshing. Not like all of these fake ass women that my mom keeps introducing me to. Anyway, I just can't stop thinking about her. I can still taste her. *Rece, get your mind right.*

I pull into my parents circular driveway and notice several cars. I guess that everyone is on time, except for me. Purposely, of course.

My parents live in our most elegant, gated sub-division called *The Ellington Estates*. Each home sits on two-plus acres of land, that backs onto a fabulous golf course. All of the homes are custom made and start at 12.5 million dollars. My parent's home is an absolutely stunning tudor-style home. My father spent nearly two years building this dream. With well over 18,000 square feet, it is perfect for entertaining…something my parents love to do. However, my dad's real talent is that he has an amazing eye for what material looks best together. He used the perfect blend of rubbed brick, stucco and timber detailing to create the perfect exterior.

After the house was completed, my mom hired some of Nashville's best interior designers to really bring their home to life. If I must say so, it is by far my dad's best work. How many people can say that they live in the subdivision which they designed and own? My favorite part of the house is the pavilion. During football season, my family literally camps out there. It's the perfect man space. We can watch football, cook, drink and sleep. Every man's fantasy.

I open the front door and immediately hear voices and laughter. I notice that everyone has gathered in the living room.

"There he is. My darling son." My mom says, as she walks towards me and kisses me on the cheek. She is still incredibly stunning at sixty. "You're late." She snaps in my ear, while keeping her lovely smile.

"Yeah, yeah. I'm here aren't I?" I kiss her back and greet everyone.

"Mr. and Mrs. Goldstein," I shake Mr. Goldstein's hand and kiss Mrs. Goldstein on the cheek.

"Hi, Dad," I say, as I step towards my father.

"Hi, son." We give each other our usual hug.

"Son, you do remember the Goldstein's beautiful daughter, Heather?"

"Hello, Heather." I kiss her on the cheek. She blushes.

"Hello, Rece. Nice to see you, again." She says while attempting to push her boobs out even more. As if that's what I'm interested in. God, she's irritating.

"You, too." I lie. Heather looks like she's had a nose job since I last saw her, but she's dressed very nice. She's wearing a beautiful silk, striped Escada dress and some Brian Atwood pumps. She does have one thing going for her, she always wears clothes that are quite flattering. Even with the boobs.

I excuse myself so that I can say hello to Mindy and Bronson. Mindy is such a beautiful person, both inside and out. She reminds me of a younger Julia Roberts.

"Hi, guys."

"Hey, Rece. How's my favorite brother-in-law?" Mindy asks, while giving me a hug.

"Shit, pour me a glass of whatever you guys are drinking."

We all laugh because they know Mom is a piece of work.

"Oh, Rece, don't mind Mom. She'll get the message sooner or later." Bronson says.

"Hopefully sooner, huh?" Mindy chuckles.

Bronson pats me on the back, "Listen, dude, do what I did. Find you a nice woman, elope and call it a day."

"I wish it were that easy, but you know that it would kill Mom to have both of her sons elope. You know that she wants to plan *the* ultimate wedding. Now, I couldn't take away from her? Could I?" I ask.

"I understand, but in the long run it's less stress." Bronson replies.

"Yeah, you're right. Maybe I'll get lucky one day, and find someone as lovely as Mindy. Even though I don't know what the hell she saw in you." I lightly punch Bronson in the arm.

"Oh, you're making me blush." Mindy says.

"Seriously, it's rough being single." I say.

"What about your new friend?" Bronson asks.

"Gee, can't a guy have any privacy in this family?"

"No!" They both say in unison.

We laugh.

"My new friend is ummm, a breath of fresh air." I feel myself turning red.

"Well, she at least has you blushing. That's a plus." Bronson chimes in.

"Enough about me, how's the adoption coming along?"

"It's going well. The visit was nice and we are hoping to have a little one by Thanksgiving." Mindy says.

You can see the excitement on both of their faces.

"Cool! I can't wait to be an uncle."

Mindy walks into the living room and Bronson turns to me and says, "You aren't getting off the hook that easy with me. Tell me about this new friend."

"Well, there's not a whole lot to tell just yet. She's absolutely stunning, beautiful smile, smart, funny, everything."

Laughing, Bronson says, "Nothing to tell, huh?" Shaking his head. "Okay, but remember that your younger brother has to give the final thumbs up."

"I know." I reply. We tap fists.

Our mom announces that dinner is ready, and so we all head into the formal dining room, which is beautifully decorated in cream and gold. Mom even has fresh cream roses draped around the chandelier. I smile. That's my mom. She's a pain in the ass sometimes, but when it comes to entertaining she is *"The Queen"*.

Everyone has been strategically seated. I pull Heather's chair out, and then sit next to her. My brother winks at me and then smiles. I could punch him right now. Oh well, he's just being my baby brother.

I glance at the elegant printed dinner menu, and that takes away a little bit of the pain that I have to withstand this evening.

Won Ton Baskets Supreme
Mushroom Hazelnut Salad
Vichyssoise Soup
Lime and Basil Sorbet
Roasted Rack of Lamb
Parisienne Potatoes
Coffee Tortoni with Kahlua

At least I'll have a wonderful meal. Let's get this over with.

CHAPTER 14

Dinner wasn't as bad as I anticipated. I left before giving anyone an opportunity to make any outlandish remarks concerning me and Heather. During dinner I made polite conversation. At one point, Heather asked if I would be interested in getting together for dinner at a later date. I respectfully declined, and excused myself from the party a few moments later. It was apparent that she and her family were insulted that I was leaving, but I am positive that the Goldsteins will not have any problems hooking Heather up with another eligible bachelor. It's not my problem.

My mom apologized to everyone and followed me to the front door. Once there, she had a few choice words for me, but I simply laughed, kissed her on the cheek and told her that I loved her. Of course that only infuriated her even more. I'll give her a few days to cool off. Anyway, enough of that. I want to talk to Willow. I reach for my cell phone and quickly dial her number. I hope that it's not too late. She picks up after two rings.

"Hello."

"Hi there." I respond, while trying to control my smile.

"Hey you, what's happening?" She asks.

"Thinking of you." I say, boldly.

"Me, too." She responds.

"Really?" I'm a little shocked, but happy at her response.

"Yeah. I was hoping to hear from you, but I knew that you had the whole dinner thing. By the way, how was it?"

"Boring. I was thinking of you the entire time."

"Were you now?" Willow asks, inquisitively.

"Yes I was…, and I still am." I pause slightly, trying to get my nerve up. "Willow?"

"Yes." She replies softly.

"I want to see you."

"Well, come on." She says without an ounce of hesitation.

"I'm on my way."

CHAPTER 15

Willow, you have lost your mind. Leave this man alone. Are you forgetting that he is W-H-I-T-E? And your parents are going to disown you when they find out. I can't talk any sense into you. Alright, a hard head makes a soft ass!

I'm upstairs when the door bell rings, so I dash down the stairs to greet Rece. He looks fabulous in his taupe-colored Armani suit, with a crisp, striped shirt that's slightly exposing his muscular chest. He smiles and steps into the foyer. *Mmmm, he smells good.*

"Hi, Rece."

He doesn't say anything, he just grabs me, pulls me towards him and kisses me. Soft at first, and then our mouths explode with a mind blowing intensity. Hot, sweltering, on fire! We both moan. I can feel his hands on my ass. *Damn, his hands feel good!* I run my fingers through his hair and across his broad shoulders. *Lord Jesus, help me. Please! But, I really don't want this feeling to stop. It's been so long since someone has kissed me like this, and I'm loving it!*

"Whew!" he says, while leaning back. "You taste good."

I'm blushing, and trying to catch my breath. "Would you like some wine?"

"Yeah, I think I need a glass." He says, while running his hand across his mouth.

Rece follows me into the living room, where I pour us both a glass of wine. He removes his jacket and we both get comfortable on the sofa. We spend a few minutes just looking at each other, and listening to the music of Wil Downing. We are like two teenagers. It's fun and exciting.

"So, Rece, tell me about the dinner." I ask, while pulling my feet up under me.

Rece laughs, and then leans back and rubs his head. "Man, it was torture, but the food was good." He smiles that breathtaking smile. "I really want to apologize, but this dinner was planned without my input, and I promised my mom that I would show up. Please forgive me."

"Don't mention it. I just appreciate you telling me about it. You didn't have to do that you know."

"Yeah, I know. But, I don't want to start this friendship off with secrets and lies."

"Well, thank you. I can appreciate that." *Two points for his openness.*

"But, in all seriousness, this was the last matchmaking dinner that I'm attending."

"Oh, your mom is probably like most mothers. She just wants the very best for her son. Now you can't hold that against her." I say, trying to ease his apparent frustration.

"That's true. I know that my mom loves me, but I can handle my own love life." He appears exasperated just talking about it.

"Parents. You gotta love 'em." I reply with a comforting tone.

We nod in agreement.

"Well, my mom semi-drilled me about you Mr. Gallantine."

"Did she now?" He leans a little towards me.

"Yeah, but it was cool. No biggie. I expect that from my mom, but my dad just asked if I had a good time, and left it at that."

"Fathers are generally that way." Rece says.

"You're right about that."

Rece takes a long sip of wine, and then looks at me somewhat seriously.

"Did you tell your parents that I am white?"

"Are you white?" I kid in my best dumb blond accent. "Damn, I totally missed that!" I laugh.

"Oh, you got jokes?" He tries to contain his laughter, but it doesn't work.

"Just kidding. And no, I didn't mention your race to my parents." I ponder his reaction, but he seems quite chilled.

"Well, do you think it will be a problem?"

"Let's just say that they will be shocked." I take a sip of wine and stretch my legs out.

"Well, in all honesty, my mom is going to hit the roof." He chuckles.

"Really? Can you handle that?" I ask.

"I can handle it." He says, with a tone of assuredness.

"Okay, if you say so, Mr. Gallantine." I reply, though I don't know if I'm really convinced, but we'll see.

"I say so." He says, while reaching out to caress my feet.

"Cool."

Rece moves closer. He places my legs across his, takes my hand and kisses the palm. "How about we take this friendship one day at a time, and if it evolves into something, we'll make formal introductions. Until then, let's just enjoy getting to know each other. Will that work for you, Miss James?"

"That will work." I reply, as we lift our glasses and toast.

SIX MONTHS LATER

CHAPTER 16

It's Friday afternoon and I'm just finishing up with one of my clients. I find myself drifting off while she's speaking because she is beyond warped. I am so happy that this is our last session. I have been coaching Carmen Steller for nearly a year. Well, I have been her personal therapist for nearly a year. What started off as something quite positive, has turned into Carmen loading all of her insecurities into my lap and her failing to recognize how she plays a large role in how her life has turned out. Here's her story:

Carmen Steller is a forty year-old, single, very dark skinned black woman. She is average looking and has had multiple plastic surgeries in an effort to look more white. Her father left her mother when she was a child, and she developed this hatred toward all black men because of him. Also, while attending Tennessee State University, she felt like she was always overlooked by the guys on the campus for girls that were light-skinned, with long hair. As a result of these experiences, she only dates white men and believes that all black men are dogs. I have tried to get her to see that her experiences were just isolated incidences, and that there are wonderful black men in this world, but she isn't hearing it.

Carmen has such low self-esteem, and she doesn't even see it. I feel so sorry for her, but I just can't continue these sessions.

"Carmen, I really thought we were making progress, and that you have now opened yourself up to the possibility of dating a black man." I say.

"Girl, I thought about it, and thought about it some more, and I just can't do it. I just don't like black men. They're just a bunch of scrubs!" She replies.

"Wow!" I'm utterly amazed. I shake my head in disgust.

She stands and walks towards the bay window in my office. As she's staring out of the window, she says something that blows my mind. "Plus, I gotta have a pretty baby, with good hair!"

"What?" I exclaim.

"You heard me. I ain't about to give birth to no nappy-headed child." She turns towards me, and then sits on the ledge of the window.

"Carmen, having a baby by a white man is not going to guarantee you having an attractive baby, or a baby with a nice grade of hair." I'm boiling on the inside. How dare her?

"Humph…say what you want, but I'll take my chances."

Uncrossing my legs I lean forward. "Carmen, it really saddens me that you still have this much self-loathing going on inside of you."

"Wait just a minute! How many times do I have to tell you that I don't hate myself." She says, with an attitude.

"Carmen, it's evident in everything you do. You've had numerous procedures to make yourself look less black. You only socialize with white people. You only date white men, and you shun anything that is remotely black. If that's not self-hate I don't know what is." I say, while massaging my temples.

"Listen, Willow. You haven't been through what I've been through. Look at you, you're beautiful. You had boyfriends in college. Brothas didn't give me the time of day. You had to be light, bright, or damn near white. To top that, my dad left my mother for some light-skinned chick. I have just had enough. I'm tired of being overlooked by brothas." She sighs, while tears run down her cheeks.

"Carmen, your father leaving your mother for a light-skinned woman didn't have anything to do with you. Sure it hurt, but it wasn't about you. A couple of brothas on TSU's yard dissed you. So what? You aren't the first woman to be rejected. Get over it! Also, carrying all of this around for this long, and piling all black men into one category is just wrong. There are good black men. I know several. Sure, some have issues, but so do men in every race. You have got to get over this and start loving yourself. Right now you don't, and that's real talk." I say, while handing her a tissue.

Carmen sits in silence for a while before responding. "Willow, I know what you're saying is right, but I just can't seem to let go of the hurt."

I grab her hand. "You do it one day at a time." Pausing for a moment to allow her to get her composure. "Have you been doing your self-love exercises?"

She shakes her head.

"Maybe it's time to start. You can't love someone fully, or have someone love you, until you love you. Understand?"

"Yes." She replies.

"Well, this is our last session. I hope that I have helped you in some way and that these sessions have been enriching."

"They have, Willow. You are the best. Brutally honest, but the best."

We laugh.

"Take care, Carmen, and the best of luck with everything you do." We hug and I walk her to the door. I watch her get into her car and we wave goodbye.

"Whew! I am glad that's over. She is a basket case. Shit, I need therapy after talking to her. Now I see why she doesn't have any friends, or the ones that she has are just as dysfunctional as she is." I say out loud, as I step back into my home. I walk back into my office, and sit in my leather chair just to clear my mind before my next session. I close my eyes for a moment, and then my phone rings.

"Good afternoon. *The Right Path*, how may I help you?"

"Hi, sweetheart."

"Hi, Rece. How are you?"

"I'm good. What are you up to?"

"I just finished my last session with Carmen."

"Crazy Carmen?" He asks, while laughing.

"Yes, and she is as crazy as ever."

"She still wants a white man, huh?" He asks.

"Yes." I reply, while chuckling.

"You should let me hook her up with one of my boys."

"No way! You do not want to put *that* on anyone. Trust me."

"You're right. My boys would never forgive me."

In agreement we both say, "Never."

"We still on for tonight?" He asks.

"Of course we are." I reply.

"My place, eight o'clock."

"I wouldn't miss it." I purr.

"I love you, Willow."

"Me, too." I reply with a smile.

CHAPTER 17

I can't believe it's been six months since Willow and I started dating. I must say, this ride has been incredibly refreshing. Willow is truly a breath of fresh air. I love seeing her, hearing her voice, loving her. I can't recall ever feeling this way towards anyone. Sure, I've dated lots of women, and I've cared deeply for quite a few, but nothing comes close to what I feel towards Willow. We've seen each other nearly every day, and have experienced the most romantic times together. All without sex. I know, I'm in shock too, but to be perfectly honest, I'm glad that we've waited. This way has allowed us a chance to really get to know each other for who we are and *not* for what we could get from each other. I truly love her. I've learned so much from her. Our latest venture was wine tasting. I knew a little bit about wine, but Willow is a true sommelier.

We just got back from the Virginia Wine Festival where we picked up some fabulous Petit Verdot and Riesling. We plan on going to Sonoma Valley in the spring. I love the fact that she is well-traveled and well-versed on so many subject matters. I credit her parents for exposing her to so many cultures. We both have traveled the world, but my trips were mostly site seeing ventures. Willow fully immersed herself in the various cultures by staying with native families to get a full understanding of the people, and their culture. I wish I would have done something like that. Her parents wanted her experiences to go far beyond the surface.

Oh yeah, the parents. Neither of us has met each others parents, but I plan on bringing Willow to my parents' home on Thanksgiving. I; however, will be meeting Willow's family this weekend. I'm a little nervous, but I welcome the opportunity to meet her mom and dad. It's time. I did meet her best friend, Journey, a few weeks ago. She seemed to ease up off me after about an hour of interrogation. Believe me, she drilled me. I also introduced Willow to my brother, Bronson. He and his wife had us over for dinner. It was very nice. Bronson and Mindy immediately liked Willow. *Which is a rarity.* They have both been sworn to secrecy and can't tell Mom or Dad. It is wearing Bronson out having to keep this to himself. He says that Mom is going to flip out when she meets Willow. He's right, but she'll get over it. Right now, I am just going to relish in this wonderful moment, and prepare for a most romantic evening with the love of my life.

CHAPTER 18

I pull up to the gate, punch in my security code and slowly drive up the winding road. Whew! Tonight's the night. I am finally giving up the coochie cat to Rece. I am nervous, excited and scared. Scared that I am taking another chance on love, and that I am opening my heart up to another man. Not that I never thought I would love again. It's just that I never imagined it being Rece. I can't really put into words what I feel towards him. He's kind, gentle, sensitive, strong and funny. Plus, he's fine as hell, and has a big dick. *Now, you know I had to at least touch it before I took the final leap.* So, all that talk about white boys being inferior in the penis department is definitely a myth, because Mr. Rece Gallantine is packing! Now, I'll just have to see how he works his tool of steel. God, please let him be fabulous. I couldn't stand it if he wasn't. I mean, the way this man kisses me and touches me, is amazing. He finger-fucked me two nights ago, and I thought I would die from ecstasy. Mmmm, I'm getting wet just thinking about him. I pull in front of Rece's place, grab my bag and step out of my car. As I'm walking towards the front door, I glance up at the midnight sky. The stars seem especially bright tonight. I take two deep breaths before ringing the doorbell. *Okay chicka, no turning back now...*

CHAPTER 19

Rece opens the door wearing a gray, long-sleeved, jersey knit top, with matching drawstring pants. I love the way the jersey hugs his tight body. We exchange kisses, and Rece grabs my bag and places it on the floor. My nose is immediately drawn to the aroma of something fabulous. He grabs my hand and leads me into the softly lit dining room. His rococo-inspired dining room table and beautifully patterned leather chairs really make this room. Not to mention the imported ornate light fixtures. He has excellent taste. I gasp. The room is breathtaking. "Oh, Rece, it's beautiful." I say, while Rece pulls out a chair for me to sit down. I have always loved Rece's place. He designed everything, and his formal dining area exudes nothing but warmth. From the chocolate-colored walls, to the unique, step ceiling. The dining room has rear views that overlook the entire city of Nashville. In the center of the room sits a beautiful, custom-made mahogany dining table, accented with oversized leather chairs, with nail head decorative trims. A two-sided fireplace is shared between the dining and living area. Tonight, Rece has placed oddly shaped water vases throughout both rooms with water lilies floating in each. There are candles flickering everywhere, with the soft scent of sandalwood. It's so romantic.

"Thank you. I wanted everything to be special." He says, and then kisses me softly on the top of my head. Rece grabs the bottle of Sauvignon Blanc and fills both our glasses. He sits next to me and says, "Let's toast."

"What shall we toast to?" I ask.

"You decide." He replies.

"Mmmm. How about to a very romantic evening?"

"That will definitely work."

We lift our glasses and toast.

Just as our glasses tap, I hear a noise coming from the kitchen. I start to ask Rece who is in the kitchen, when out walks Chef Jazz. Chef Jazz is one of the most popular chefs on television. His specialty is seafood cuisine. The things this man can do with lobster is absolutely amazing. He's a large, handsome man, the color of chocolate silk. You can tell that he enjoys his cooking, too. He has a closely-cropped goatee that adds a sense of charm. His salt and pepper hair is wavy. He instantly reminds you of a dark Duke Ellington.

"Well, good evening, pretty lady." He says, with a brown sugar Southern drawl, while placing a napkin on my lap. "I'm Chef Jazz." He smiles and extends his hand.

"Hello, I'm Willow." I reply, with a surprised look towards Rece. He chuckles as if he's reading my mind.

"Miss Willow, you must be a mighty special lady to get ol' Chef to cook for you on a Friday evening. Cuz Friday is poker night with the fellas, but Rece here wouldn't take no for an answer." Chef Jazz lets out a hearty laugh, and pats Rece on the shoulder and places his napkin.

"Well then, I feel extra special. I'm flattered that you'd give up poker night for me." I reply.

Rece interjects, "Sweetheart, don't let him fool you. He loves cooking for pretty women."

"Now, that I do!" Chef Jazz quickly responds.

We all burst into a hearty laugh.

"Now, shoosh and enjoy one of the best meals you'll ever eat."

Chef Jazz excuses himself, and Rece and I quickly dive into our baby spinach salads with seared shrimp, bacon and roasted bell peppers. It is absolutely divine. Chef Jazz enters the room again and tells us to just ignore him while he places an array of foods before us. After arranging the last platter, Chef Jazz walks towards me and places a gentle kiss on my hand. "Have a wonderful evening, Miss Willow, I'm outta here. It was a pleasure meeting you."

"Likewise." I reply.

Rece stands. "Thanks, Jazz."

They shake hands and embrace.

"Anytime, man." Chef replies.

Rece walks Chef to the front door, and then returns and sits next to me. I lean over and kiss him softly.

He runs his fingers across his lips. "Wow, what's that for?" He asks.

"Just for tonight." Pausing for a moment. "This is really nice, Rece."

"If you think this is nice, just wait until later."

"Really?"

"Yes, really."

We chuckle and blush at the thought of what the night will bring.

"All of this looks really good. Where should we start?" Rece asks.

I grab one of the spice-dusted scallops and feed it to Rece.

"Now, that's really delicious." Rece says.

"Let me taste." I say, as I lean forward and kiss Rece, again. I taste the cumin and curry. "Mmmm, spicy." I softly speak.

"Yes, you are." He whispers.

"Stop it!" I coyly exclaim.

"Hey, you're the one who keeps coming over here messing with me." He says, while running his finger down the center of my chest.

I laugh. "You're right. Let's eat. I would hate to waste a meal made by Chef Jazz."

"Me, too."

We spend the next hour feeding each other the best seafood anyone could ever imagine. Between the kissing, finger sucking and chin licking, we somehow manage to finish our meal.

CHAPTER 20

After dinner, Rece takes my hand and we follow a trail of rose petals that lead to his bedroom upstairs. He opens the French doors, and I immediately notice the white rose petals covering his mink bedspread. I smile. The mellow sound of Miles Davis is playing softly, and the flicker of candles are bouncing off of the blue, muted walls. Rece's room is masculine, yet soft. He's chosen big, dark wooden furniture. The California king fits comfortably in this large space. His windows are bare, allowing the natural glow from the moon and stars to fill the room resulting in the most romantic ambience known to man. The mink bedspread is accented with several chocolate brown and blue pillows, covered in various prints and patterns. Unique sculptures from his travels are also dispersed throughout the room. An original Georgia O'Keeffe hangs above his headboard. This is indeed a romantic paradise.

I walk towards the bed and sit down. I take my hand and run my fingers through the soft petals. "Rece, you've thought of everything." I say.

"Are you sure?" He asks. "I wanted tonight to be special."

"I'm positive. I love how you always pay attention to the details."

"I try." Rece says, while joining me on the bed. He takes my hand and places it between his and says, "You are so beautiful, and I love you with all of my heart."

"I love you, too, Rece." I start to tear up.

"What's wrong, baby?" Rece asks with care, while wiping away a tear.

"Oh, it's nothing. I'm just really happy that you're a part of my life."

"Well, the feelings are mutual, Willow. I thank God for you every day. You are my blessing."

"Oh, Rece, I love you." I reply.

We kiss.

Rece gently falls back on the bed and pulls me on top of him. He looks at me for a moment, while running his fingers through my hair. I lean forward, take my tongue and softly lick his lips. Back and forth. Back and forth. I suck his top lip, and then his bottom lip, never allowing my tongue to enter his mouth. I just want to enjoy his lips. I then take my tongue and make a trail down to his clean shaven, cleft chin and begin to suck. I suck his chin as if it's a short, thick dick. He moans. I know that he's imagining this sensation on his own rod of passion. I can feel his hands slip up under my loosely-fitted silk dress. He starts massaging my ass. His hands are strong and slightly callus. No doubt from the many years of construction work. I know that I am being touched by a man. I move my hips to acknowledge his touch, while making a trail back up to his mouth. This time he opens his mouth and our tongues dance a hard, hot tango. The kiss is volcanic.

I feel Rece lifting my hips, allowing me to straddle him. I'm not wearing any panties, so when I lower my ass I feel Rece's hard dick pulsing through his jersey knit pants. I begin swaying my hips back and forth to allow my pussy to gently brush up against his steel rod. He lifts his hips to meet my dark, wet heaven. We both moan in unison. I lift my head and our eyes lock. Without saying a word, Rece lifts my dress over my head. I reach for him and he grabs my hands.

"No, let me enjoy. "He says, while caressing both of my breasts and using his thumbs to gently massage my hardened nipples. I squirm with delight. Then Rece grabs my breasts, and begins playing the most wonderful symphony on my nipples. I am not typically a breast woman when it comes to foreplay, but when he licked up under my breasts, and did this soft suck and gentle tug on my nipples…*oooh whee! Jesus! He can play with my titties anytime*. All the while, he is grinding between my legs and positioning his dick so that it gently taps my love castle. *Shit, I'm wet!* Rece removes his shirt, and I run my fingers across his tight chest. *God, this man is sexy!* We kiss, again. I'm touching him everywhere. He flips me onto my back and climbs between my legs. He spreads my thighs and let's his fingers brush against my pussy.

"Ahhh, just a strip. I like that shit!" He says matter-of-factly, while tracing my clit with his finger.

"Oh, baby…that feels good. Mmmm." I pant.

"Does it?" He asks.

"Yes." I whisper.

"I want to please you, Willow. I want to be your best. So, don't hold back on me baby. Tell me what you want." Rece says, while taking my legs and placing my feet on his chest. He then plants the softest kiss on each foot, before sucking each one of my toes. I chuckle with pleasure. After using my toes as an appetizer, Rece spreads my legs, again, and lowers himself so that he is eye level with my coochie. I feel him spreading my luscious pussy lips apart, and then I feel his tongue snaking up and down my inner cavern. He works his way towards my clit and introduces himself in the most erotic manner. He softens his tongue and covers my sensitive clit like a soft blanket, and then he sucks and licks it. Not hard and rigid, but a soft suck that sends incredible chills up my spine.

"Oh, Rece, that's it, baby. Shit, goddamn!" I scream.

"Yeah, baby. Talk to me…tell me what you want." Rece instructs while working my clit.

"Mmmm." I moan. I've never had anyone ask me to tell them what I like. Most men just assume and those that do happen to ask…never listen.

"How about this?" He asks, while inserting a finger into my dripping, wet pussy.

"Oh, God, yes! That's it, Rece." I say, while grabbing Rece's head and throwing my pussy into his face.

"Yeah, Willow, that's it. Let go." Rece inserts another finger, and then finds my G-spot. I scream uncontrollably.

"Ahhh! Rece, don't stop, baby!"

"I won't, baby. I'm here for you." He replies.

"Oh, Rece, fuck me with your tongue!" I yell. Rece obliges me and begins darting his tongue in and out of my pussy. The sensation is incredible. With each dart I move my hips to meet his tongue. Rece lifts my ass and proceeds to give me a rim job out of this world. I am losing my mind. Before I know it, I scream, "Play with my ass baby, put your finger in my ass!" *Shit, where did that come from? I guess I have always enjoyed having my ass played with, but scared to tell just any man, because men think that when you ask them to play with your ass it's an automatic invitation to screw you in the ass, and believe me, it's NOT. I'm not trying to get fucked in the ass!*

"Ahhh shit, that's what I'm talking about, baby. Give me this ass." Rece wets one of his fingers with my juices, and inserts it slowly into my ass. My ass relaxes with ease and enjoys the tantalizing sensation. I lose all sense of thought. Having my clit, G-spot and ass delighted all at once is beyond pleasure. It is ecstasy.

"Oh, Rece, I want to fuck you! I want to feel your dick inside of me."

"I want to fuck you, too, baby." He replies.

I lift myself up and greet Rece with a long kiss. The taste of my pussy inside of his mouth is erotic on a different level. Rece stands and unties his pants. They fall to the floor. His dick is at full attention.

The tip is blushing with redness. It's huge. I mean I knew Rece was packin', but my God, I never imagined this. His sword is at least nine to ten inches. Not to mention the girth. I can't help myself. I have got to suck this creamy treasure. But first, I just grab his cock and place it between my mocha titties, and gently move them up and down his dick. Rece, let's out a low, guttural moan.

"Sit down, baby." I say to Rece, before dropping to my knees. I grab Rece's dick with both of my hands to create a warm, firm environment, and begin gently licking his tip. With each lick I lower my mouth, allowing his dick to get wetter and wetter. All the while, I'm rotating my hands back and forth, applying soft and firm pressure. After saturating his dick, I began moving my head up and down while taking his entire dick inside of my mouth.

He screams, "Goddamn, Willow! Suck this shit, baby!"

I am turned on even more by his pleasure. I pull his ass towards me to allow his nuts to hang off of the bed, and I lick each one slowly before placing them both in my mouth. I later tease that ultra sensitive spot right beneath his penis and Rece loses it. "Ah shit, I can't take anymore of this!" He yells, while pulling me up and throwing me onto the bed. The heat between us is ravishing. Rece throws my legs apart, and then reaches into his night stand and grabs a condom and some lubricant. He places the condom on his rod, squirts some jelly on the tip of his dick and some on my heaven, and then positions his dick right at the entrance of my pussy. He moves his dick in a slow, circular motion… never fully entering my pussy…just teasing the entrance. I reach down and begin rubbing my clit. I can feel the ecstasy building up inside of me.

"Mmmm, that feels good, baby. Keep it right there." I pant.

"Right here?" He asks, while moving his dick inside me a little more.

"Yeah, right there, baby. I'm close. I'm about to come, Rece." I continue rubbing my clit, while taking in more of Rece's hard, thick dick. And then it happens. My pussy explodes all over Rece's passion. "Ahhhhhh, God. Lord Jesus. Oh, God!" I scream.

I am in a place of pure, uninhibited pleasure. I spread my legs wider to allow Rece to enter me fully. I feel my pussy stretching to accommodate his thickness. It's tight, but with each thrust my walls of love expand, and welcome this new visitor. Rece fucks me hard and long. I squeeze my pussy walls around his dick, increasing his pleasure. I feel his moment coming on strong, and so I reach between his legs and caress his balls while pounding my pussy to meet his every thrust. Rece screams and grabs my ass tight. I hold him close, and use my sugar walls to squeeze every ounce of cum from his dick. When it's over we don't say a word. We kiss and the kiss says it all. My pussy moans a sultry, quiet purr, *"Willow, keep this white boy, because this is some good shit."*

CHAPTER 21

I open my eyes and look over at Willow sleeping peacefully. My God, she is so beautiful. Every day that I spend with Willow leads me to believe that she's the one. She's everything that I could ever want, or desire in a woman. And last night----whew! It was by far the best sex that I have ever had. It was hot and wild. What made it so incredible was the fact that Willow was open and free. She told me what she wanted without hesitation. Willow is comfortable with her body, and not afraid to express it. The one thing that has always been a huge turn-off for me is when I get with a woman and she acts so fucking coy, and virginal. Nothing irritates me more than a grown ass woman acting as if she's never had sex before, or that she doesn't know how to give a blow job. Or, the ones who get all juvenile when you talk dirty to them, and then after two or three weeks of fucking, the real person comes out. Next thing you know, they're riding your dick like they're in a rodeo, and sucking your dick like its dripping gold. A complete contradiction of who they presented themselves to be.

That's why I've never taken a woman at face value. Give a woman a few drinks and stroke her pussy the right way, and the true essence of who she is will come out. Even those sanctified whores. You know, the ones who have screwed the whole NFL, and are now back in church and celibate. Shit, they are the biggest freaks. "Oh, I'm waiting for God to send me a husband before I have sex, again." Bullshit! I've had so many women say that to me it is ridiculous. Let me get this straight, we can't have sex, but you can suck my dick, or I can eat your pussy, all in the name of Jesus. Wow!

I should hold a session strictly for women and just educate them on some things. Men are very simple creatures and we don't need a whole lot, but there are some specific things that go a long way with every man. All men wish that they could say this on the first date:

- Have some self-esteem and stop being so needy. Do not depend on us to make your life complete.
- Be happy in your own space, and have some outside interests. No man wants to be up under his woman 24/7, and you shouldn't want to be up under your man all of the time.
- Learn how to cook. I mean, some stuff from scratch. Jiffy cornbread mix isn't cooking from scratch.
- Keep a clean house. Most men do not like a filthy woman.
- Shut up! Period. You do not always have to have the last word.
- Stop telling your girlfriends everything. Some things need to stay between you and your man.
- Learn how to fuck, and how to give a good blow job. There is nothing more shameful than a woman over thirty that only wants it missionary style, and doesn't know how to suck dick.

- Get yourself a good toy and start masturbating. Once you know your body, it will be easier for you to tell your partner what you desire.
- Go and buy some sexy pieces from Victoria's Secret or Frederick's of Hollywood. Every man loves to see his woman is something sexy.

I can hear the comments already. "What about what men need to do?" or "I don't need a man." These same women will always be ALONE, because they can't get out of their own way.

This is why I love Willow. Willow does Willow. What you see is what you get, but in that same breath, she isn't afraid to let a man lead. That in itself is so appealing. Wow! How did I get so lucky?

I decide to wake Willow with some soft kisses down her spine. She squirms and then I hear her giggle. I kiss her neck.

"Good morning, love." I say.

"Hi, baby." She answers.

"Did you sleep well?" I ask, while caressing her thighs.

"I did." She purrs.

"Well, how about we get dressed and head to the Franklin Country Club for some breakfast?"

"That's fine." She replies. "But first." She pauses for a moment, before grabbing my hand and placing it between her legs. She's warm and wet.

I quickly respond, "Breakfast can wait."

Chapter 22

Breakfast was delicious. The Franklin Country Club have the best omelets in town. Afterwards, I headed to my place to meet up with Journey. She is coming over so we can catch up on things. I'm still floating from last night. Rece is absolutely amazing. Ooooh, this man moves me. It is so refreshing to be in a relationship where I am honored and respected. Rece doesn't just wait for a special occasion to show me how much he cares for me. Every day he makes me feel wanted and appreciated. I must say, I am still a bit surprised by the fact that Rece is white. At first I was just allowing myself to go with the flow, but as time went by, his skin color became less of an issue. I suppose it has a lot to do with our interests. We both enjoy traveling, music, wine and exercising. We are also both huge movie buffs. More importantly, we laugh all of the time. I guess when you get down to it, color is only an issue if you allow it to be.

I hear the front door opening. It's Journey. She is the only person, other than my parents, that have a key to my place.

"Hey, girl!" I yell. "I'm in the kitchen."

Journey saunters into the kitchen wearing the most adorable yellow sundress. She looks at me with this devilish grin and says, "Hey, slut!" She places a greasy paper bag and her purse on the counter. I look at her and we both die laughing.

"Uh huh." Journey says while sniffing me.

I back away from her. "Uh huh, what?" I ask, as if I am unaware of what she means.

"Yeah, yeah. It's all over you. That freshly fucked glow!" She says.

We burst into laughter, again, and then hug each other,

"Girrrrl, can you really tell?" I ask, blushingly.

"Hell yeah, and I love it. Now tell me all about it."

"I will, but first something smells really good."

Journey reaches for the paper bag. "I picked us up some fried pies off of Jefferson Street."

"Shoot, I just finished eating breakfast, but I gotta have one. You know a sistah loves her some fried pies."

"Journey, grab us some napkins out of that drawer, and I'll pour us some milk."

Journey gets the linen napkins from the drawer and I follow her into the living room. I pick up my remote control and press play. The voice of Robin Thicke quickly surrounds the room. Journey sits on the love seat and I sit across from her on the sofa and take a bite of my hot pie. "Mmmm, this is so good."

"I know, girl, I could eat these every day, but then I'd be big as a house." Journey chuckles.

"I know that's right." I chime in agreement.

"Alright, I'm ready. Give me the dirt---the 411." Journey laughs, as she plops her feet on the ottoman.

I lean back and take another bite of my pie before saying, "Delicious---absolutely delicious. And I ain't talking about the pie."

"Get outta here, Willow!"

"No, get in here. Rece knocked the pussy out!" I say, while throwing punches.

Journey looks at me with wide eyes and says, "Bullshit! You mean to tell me that this white boy is fine, and can fuck?"

"Not only can he fuck, he's packing like a stallion, and he can eat pussy out of this world."

"Are you serious, Willow? Don't be fucking with your girl." Journey says while sitting up straight and pushing her bangs away from her face.

I scoot to the edge of the sofa. "Journey, I am serious. This man put it on me. I mean shiiiit! I am still in shock. You know how you hear all of these stories about white boys having small dicks? Well, I'm here to tell you that is some bullshit because Rece------*crap*------I can't even get it out." I fall back onto the sofa. "It was by far the best sex I have ever had."

"Better than Booker Williams?" Journey asks.

"Better." I reply, smiling.

"Better than Daniel Griggs?"

"Better." Still smiling.

"Damn, he is good."

We both laugh.

"Journey, this man asked me what I liked and what I wanted. Not many men are that comfortable with their egos. And he actually followed directions. Mmmm. It was a perfect evening." I say, before taking a sip from my glass.

Journey jumps up from the love seat and hugs me. "Yeah! Willow is back on the block."

We laugh.

"I am so happy for you, Willow. I like Rece. I, too, was a little skeptical at first, and I would prefer that you date a brotha, but more importantly, I want you to be happy. After meeting Rece, I have no doubt that he adores you. You deserve a good guy."

"Thank you, Journey. You're gonna make me cry."

Journey grabs my hand. "No, girl, I am serious. You went through a lot with Jordan. Lord knows you gave it your all. We were all disappointed that it didn't work out, especially me, considering he and Devin are best friends. I guess it just wasn't meant to be. Now, you have someone that is on the same page. It's a beautiful thing." Journey smiles.

"Yeah, now I understand what you've been telling me."

"Well, what about your parents? Aren't you guys going over to your folks house for dinner tomorrow?" She says while getting comfortable and plopping her feet on one of the big pillows.

"Yesssss." Dragging it out. I take a deep breath.

"Are you nervous?" Journey asks.

"A little. Not so much with Mom, but Dad is a whole different story. I just hope that he doesn't flip when he sees Rece."

"I think he'll be okay. Sure, he'll be shocked at first. What father wouldn't be? But, after he spends some time with Rece, it will work itself out." Journey states with confidence.

"From your mouth to God's ears." I say.

We bump fists and continue eating the rest of the fried pies. I'm going to regret eating these pies tomorrow.

What the hell, you only live once!

Chapter 23

It's a beautiful Sunday afternoon in Nashville. The sky is clear and the faint scent of evergreen is in the air. It's around four in the afternoon when I pull up to Willow's place. I must admit, I am a little anxious about today. Excited, but anxious. I mean, it's a big deal when you are meeting the "parents". I wonder how they are going to react. *Oh, Rece, you're over thinking this...it will be fine. Look at Willow. She's a wonderful woman. Her parents can't be that bad.* As I am getting out of my car, I see Willow coming out of her front door. She looks stunning. She's wearing a pair of wide-legged linen pants with a multi-colored, silk halter top. Her Jimmy Choo shoes and bag are a bright yellow, which accentuates the yellow in her top perfectly. Willow has her hair pulled back neatly in a bun, and her makeup is soft. I walk around my car and greet her with a gentle kiss. She smells sweet, like fresh baked sugar cookies.

She smiles. "Hi, babe."

"Hi, sweetheart." I reply, as I open the car door for her. I quickly walk back to the driver's side and get in. I run my hand down Willow's thigh before securing my seatbelt.

"You look nice." I say.

"Thanks, honey. You do, too," she says, while placing her hand on top of mine. Willow fastens her seatbelt and gets comfortable. "Sooo, today is the big day, huh?"

"Yeah, it is. I hope your parents like me." I say with a slight hesitation.

"Well, Mom will love you----Dad, on the other hand." Willow says, pausing slightly. "Let's just say, be surprised if he invites you into his library."

"His library?" I ask, with some uncertainty.

"Yes. If he invites you into his library, then you have a shot. If not, then forget it." Willow laughs.

"Gee, thanks, honey. That takes the pressure off." I respond while chuckling.

"Oh, babe, don't worry. Everything will go smoothly." She grabs my hand. "I promise."

"Okay, if you say so." I place the car in reverse. "Where are we headed?"

"Do you know where The Governor's Place is located?" Willow asks.

I pause a moment before answering. "Did you say, The Governor's Place?"

"Yeah, The Governor's Place. What's wrong?" Willow asks with concern.

"Mmmm, it's nothing. I just didn't know that your parents lived there."

"Well, how could you, honey? We've never discussed where my parents live." Willow says matter-of-factly.

"Yeah, I know. But..." I say.

"But, what?" Willow asks, with a look of concern. "Is there a problem?"

"No, sweetheart. It's not a problem. *I know The Governor's Place quite well. My father developed most of the homes there. Outside of my parents' home, The Governor's Place showcases some of his best work.*

"I wonder if?"

"What, babe? Wonder what?" Willow quizzes.

"Nothing. I was just thinking aloud." I squeeze her hand to reassure her.

"Okaaay. Stop being so weird and nervous. You'll do fine. Plus, I love you and that's all that really matters, right?" She asks.

"Right." I say, before taking off to The Governor's Place.

CHAPTER 24

We pull up to the tightly-guarded entrance of The Governor's Place. A guard walks up to my car as I lower the driver's side window.

"Good evening, sir. Welcome to The Governor's Place". The gentleman says, in a kind, but commanding voice. He's a large, white guy with a blond crew cut. It's obvious that he works out because his muscles are about to burst through his uniform shirt. *Why not just get a larger shirt? I just don't get guys like this. Oh, well, maybe he needs the attention.*

"Hello." I reply.

"Hi, Robert!" Willow says. The guard backs up a bit to look inside of the car.

He quickly flashes a smile. "Oh, Miss James. Nice to see you."

"You, too, Robert. By the way, this is my friend, Rece."

He extends his hand and we shake. "Hello, nice to meet you," he says with less of a command than before.

"Likewise," I reply.

Robert asks me for my driver's license, and then walks to the back of my car and writes down my license plate number. He walks back to his guard station to run my license and plates before returning to the car. It doesn't matter that I am with Willow, everyone has to get cleared before entering this exclusive subdivision. Robert hands me my license and bids us a good evening. Afterwards, he buzzes us through the gate, and we drive up the hill towards Willow's parents' home.

Willow asks that I make a quick right into a beautiful, circular driveway that is manicured with the most exquisite detail. I have only seen this type of landscape artistry once, and that's at my parents' home. I look at this breathtaking French Country estate, and I instantly know…this is my dad's work. His signature use of brick, stone and steep hip roof lines add such charm to a home. It's his mark. *Are you sure Rece? Your dad isn't the only builder of French Country homes. I'll know for sure once I step inside. Wow, I didn't know that Willow came from this type of wealth. This home is from our Signature Series which start at ten million dollars. I am just blown away. Not by the fact that she's very well off, but because she never flaunts it. Believe me, this is a rarity in the South. Most women who come from money let you know on the first date. This is why I love this woman. She is simply unlike anyone I have ever come across. Wow, this is deep.* I take a deep breath and walk around to open Willow's door. Willow steps out and gives me a soft peck on the lips.

"What's that for?" I ask.

"Because I love you," she says, while smiling. We grab hands.

"Oh, I almost forgot." I click open my trunk, and grab the floral arrangement I picked up for Willow's mom.

Willow looks at me with a slight smirk. "Fresh flowers, huh? Uh, you got two points already."

We bump fists and then burst into laughter. I reach for the comforting feel of Willow's hand and walk towards the front door.

"SOUP"

CHAPTER 25

Willow reaches into her purse, grabs a set of keys and opens the large, ornate front door. We step into the impressive, two-story foyer with its grand staircase, tray ceiling and overlooking balcony. The house is elegantly decorated in shades of blue, burgundy and cream. The dark wood accents add to the ambience. I glance to the right and notice the lovely living room area. My eyes quickly land on the Roubini sofa in an awesome navy, Prugna silk velvet. Wow, it's exquisite. From the foyer I can see into the kitchen, and that's when all of my thoughts are confirmed. I see a stainless steel LaCornue range. LaCornue is France's premiere, high-end culinary range. My dad uses this range upon special request by his exclusive clients. *Damn! My dad built this house. How ironic is this?*

"Willow…baby, is that you?" A pleasant voice echoes from the kitchen.

"Yes, Mom, it's me." Willow grabs my hand and chuckles as we head towards the kitchen.

"Come on back, dear, I'm in the kitchen." Her mom replies.

Willow's mom is grabbing a dish from the oven. She turns to place the delicious smelling entrée on the island

and looks up. She is stunning. I instantly see where Willow gets her good looks from. Mrs. James stands about five feet eight inches. She's about two shades lighter than Willow, and has a fabulous short cut that flatters her salt and pepper hair color. I can tell that she takes good care of herself by her toned, muscular arms. Mrs. James takes off her oven mitts and apron, and walks towards us. She greets Willow with a kiss.

"Hi, Willow!" She says.

"Hi, Mama." Willow replies.

Mrs. James looks towards me and reaches out to shake my hand. "You must be Rece." She says with a sense of warmth.

"Yes, ma'am, I am." I respond with a smile.

"Well, pleased to meet you," She says, while patting my hand.

"Likewise. Oh, these are for you." I say, while handing her the bouquet of flowers.

She smiles. "Ohhh, did Willow tell you how much I love fresh flowers?"

"No, ma'am."

"Well, I do! Thank you Rece. This is very thoughtful."

'No problem. Mrs. James it's my pleasure." I say.

Willow smiles and says, "Mom, Rece is always thoughtful."

"Good. It's a great trait to have." She says, while reaching for a vase. "Rece, make yourself at home."

"Thanks, Mrs. James. By the way, you have a lovely home."

Continuing to arrange her flowers, she replies, "Thank you. We like it."

"Mom, where is Daddy?" Willow asks, while taking a swipe of icing off of the cake sitting at the edge of the island. "Mmmm, this is good."

"He's on a business call. Heeeeey, get away from that cake." Mrs. James says, while throwing the dish towel at Willow. "That's for dessert!"

"Ohhh, just one more taste." Willow laughs, while taking another swipe of icing. "Come on, Rece, before I get into trouble." Willow says, while still laughing.

"Yeah, get on outta here. There's fresh lemonade in the pavilion," she says, while shaking her head. "Fix Rece a glass."

"Yes, Mama." Willow replies, as we walk out of the French doors onto the pavilion. The voice of Nina Simone is echoing softly through the outdoor speakers. Willow and I make ourselves comfortable on one of the cushioned sofas.

I lean back slightly and rub my hands together.

"You okay, honey?" She asks.

"Yeah, babe, I'm fine." I reply.

"Good. I want you to feel at home." She says, while running her hand down my thigh.

I turn and look at Willow. "Your mom seems really nice."

"She is. I wouldn't trade her for the world, but she can be a mess at times."

"Well, I see where you get your good looks from." I say, while touching Willow's chin.

Willow nudges me. "Don't be trying to flirt with my mom."

We both laugh.

"Uhhh, I don't know. She's pretty hot." Laughing.

"Yeah, she is. Mom takes really good care of herself, plus she and Dad are really active."

"Now, I know what you'll look like when we're old and gray." I smile, while placing Willow's hand in mine.

She returns the smile. "Oh, will you now?" We kiss softly.

"Yes."

"We'll see if you can hang." Willow nudges me.

"Oh, I can hang." I reply.

We both crack up. Willow stands and walks towards the dining table.

"You want some lemonade?" She asks.

"Sure, babe. That would be nice." I reply.

As Willow is reaching for the crystal pitcher, her father walks out. *Okay Rece, it's going to be alright. Be cool. Be calm.*

"Hi, Daddy." Willow smiles as she reaches out to give her dad a hug. I can see the love that she has for him. It radiates.

"Hi, baby." He replies, while hugging her tightly before turning his attention towards me. His eyes are not welcoming.

Mr. James instantly commands his space. He is a tall, statuesque man with a handsome, chiseled face. He's wearing a light blue, Tommy Bahama linen shirt, with a pair of khaki linen pants. He looks at me with an intense stare. I stand to greet him. Willow walks back over to where I am standing, and places her hand in the small of my back. Excitedly she says, "Daddy, this is---------."

"I'll be goddamned!" Shaking his head from side to side. "Willow, I know you didn't bring a white boy up in my house!"

I feel Willow's hand squeeze the small of my back. I'm still in shock.

"Yes, Daddy…this is Rece, and Rece, this is my dad." She says sweetly.

I extend my hand, but Mr. James doesn't move.

Not quite sure of what I should do, I decide to speak instead. "Uhh…hi, Mr. James, uh, it's a pleasure to meet you, sir."

"Shiiiit, you're white." He says matter-of-factly, with a huge air of disdain.

"Well, that I am sir." I reply nervously in utter disbelief.

Mr. James starts pacing back and forth. It's obvious he's in shock. "I can't believe this shit!" He screams.

"Walter, stop being so rude." Mrs. James says, while walking quickly towards us.

"Wil, our daughter; my sweet little girl brought a cracker up in my house!"

"Yes, she did. Since that's out of the way, now we can enjoy our evening." Mrs. James pats him on the behind and laughs. *I don't know what the hell is going on, but I am not saying a word. If I didn't love Willow, I would curse her father out about now. What the fuck?*

"Shit, I don't know about this." He says, before turning to me and saying, "Rece, you see that door over there?"

"Yes, sir." I reply.

"That's my wine cellar. Go down there and pick us a bottle to go with our steaks. If you pick a good one, I might let your white ass stay. Now, go on." He says, while pointing towards the cellar. Willow breaks into a small smirk and then winks. I give her a look that says, "This is some bullshit!" before heading towards the door. As I am walking away, I can hear Willow and her mom trying to set Mr. James straight, but I have a feeling they are not going to win this battle. This is certainly not what I expected. I mean, I knew that her parents might be in somewhat of a shock, but I never imagined her dad verbalizing his feelings in such a manner. Oh well, I'm in it to win it. I open the cellar door and retreat down the flight of stairs. As I open the wrought iron door, I let my eyes take in the massive cellar. God, this has to hold at least three thousand bottles of wine. I would love to spend a few hours in here, but I am not here for pleasure. Luckily, the wines are categorized. "Mmmm, I think I'll settle on a Cabernet. Nah, what about a Pinot Noir? *Rece, it has to be an excellent choice.* Ahhh, this is it."

I pull the bottle of Andrew Hardy "The Ox" Shiraz down from the shelf. *Excellent*! I had this wine once when I traveled to Australia. I like it because it has strong hints of chocolate, with lovely underlying black pepper, perfect with red meat. I've tried for years to get my hand on a bottle, but came up short. There were only seventy cases of the 2003 vintage produced. Mr. James has four bottles in his collection. He has to be connected to have gotten his hands on these. *He'll be surprised that I know about this wine, plus I want him to splurge for calling me a cracker.* I laugh to myself.

I close the door to the cellar, and walk back to join Willow and her parents. I gather from the look on everyone's face that they're still discussing me. I walk up to Mr. James, and hand him the bottle of wine that I selected.

"Will this do, sir?" I ask.

Mr. James takes the bottle of wine from me and smiles slightly. "I see you know a little something about wine?" He inquires.

"Uh, a little bit, sir." I respond modestly.

"Whatcha' know about Andrew Hardy?"

"Well, actually I tasted it when I took a trip to Australia. I haven't been able to get my hands on a bottle since; at least not until today." I smile.

Mr. James extends his arm and we finally shake hands. Willow and her mom look at each other and smile.

"Well, Rece, you might be okay. I mean you know a good wine, that's for sure. But, let's not get ahead of ourselves. We'll see how the rest of the evening goes."

"That's fine with me, sir." I reply with relief.

"Rece, don't mind Walter. He's just giving you a hard time, sweetie." Mrs. James says.

"Yeah, honey, my dad really is a nice guy." Willow says, while giving me a hug.

"Shiiit, Rece don't believe these women. I'm mean as hell and don't you forget it! Now, let's eat."

CHAPTER 26

Dinner turned out to be quite enjoyable. I really didn't know what to make of Mr. James, but he proved to be a man of great interest. Willow's parents are incredibly down- to-earth, and have great senses of humor. Not to mention, Mrs. James is a great cook. I can officially go on record stating that I have never tasted a more delicious carrot cake. Mrs. James promised that she'd pack me a few slices to take home.

After dinner, Willow and her mom started cleaning off the table, and Mr. James invited me to his study for a nightcap. As soon as he offered, Willow pinched me and smiled. I couldn't help but smile to myself. I knew this meant that he thought I had some potential with his daughter. *Wow! This is big. Good job, Rece*! Mr. James and I walk through the kitchen and down the long hallway. Beautiful, original art by Ernie Barnes adorn the walls. His study is the perfect man's retreat. Dark, rich colors, all accented by fine wood and plush leather, make the room quite comfortable. Custom shelving showcases lovely family photos and his numerous awards for his contributions in the field of education. Mr. James is a remarkable man. I mean, here is someone that was born into poverty and is now one of the most sought after experts in the field of education. He has set up educational systems in eight third-world countries. He is incredibly intelligent, and yes…outspoken. He does not bite his tongue, but I can respect a man that speaks his mind.

Mr. James walks toward his minibar and pours us each a glass of scotch. As he is pouring, he asks me to go over by the shelving and push a protruding, silver button. I push the button and step back as a custom built humidor appears.

"Wow! This is nice, Mr. James." I say, while trying to take in all of the variety of cigars this humidor is showcasing.

"Thanks, Rece." He replies. "You smoke, son?"

"Uh, I enjoy a nice cigar every blue moon. I've had some good ones through my travels, but I'd like to learn a bit more because I do enjoy a good smoke."

"Cool. Pick out a couple." Mr. James laughs.

"You trust me on this?" I ask, hesitantly.

"Shiiit, if you pick cigars like you pick wine then you're in like Flynn."

We both laugh. Mr. James places our glasses on the large, wooden table and then sits in one of the masculine leather chairs. He grabs a leather box off of the small, light stand and opens it. Inside are his cigar tools. I'm not close to him, but I can tell that his tools are top of the line. He pulls out the cutter and the torch, and places them on the table between our drinks. *I am really digging this humidor.*

"If you don't mind me asking, sir, who designed your humidor?"

"Actually, the guy that designed it is also the guy I get my cigars from. His name is Scott. He owns a smoke shop in Mount Juliet called the Cigar Lounge. Real cool dude and a nice spot. Stop by there when you have some time. Tell him you know me, and he'll set you up."

"Thanks, I'll do that."

Mr. James claps his hands once and rubs them together. "Whatcha' got for me, Rece, my boy!" He says, while laughing. I walk over and hand him a couple of Partagas Piramides Le 2000. They're a full-bodied torpedo. I've had them a few times and I loved them. Thank goodness he had something I was familiar with.

"Ahhh, Rece my man…you might be alright."

We both let out a hearty laugh and bump fists. "This is a good cigar. Do you prefer a torpedo?" He inquires.

"I like this particular torpedo, but I haven't had enough of them to compare, and I don't know enough to even know where to start. To be perfectly honest, I just started smoking." I reply sincerely.

"Well," Mr. James gets up and walks towards his humidor. He pulls out one of the drawers, and grabs a small stainless steel box and places a few cigars inside before handing it to me. "Ok, these are pretty good. They are Graycliff Originals. It's another nice, full-bodied cigar. If you like these, I'll put you up on something even better."

I smile. I am truly flattered. I can't believe that this is the same cat that went off on me. "Thank you, sir, I appreciate this." I pause while admiring the stainless, cedar-lined, monogrammed box. "Custom cigar boxes, huh?"

Mr. James cuts both cigars and hands me one. He lights them both before saying, "Son, don't ever do anything half-assed. If you're gonna do it, do it like it's never been done." Looking at me with a serious stare. "Understand?" He asks.

"Yes, sir, I do." I say, before taking a sip from my glass.

He takes a long drag before resting his cigar in the ash tray. "Rece, I'm gonna be honest with you, son."

"You mean, you're gonna start now?" I chuckle.

"You got me," he laughs. "Well, as you have probably figured out; I don't cut corners."

"True." I respond.

"Now, to be perfectly candid with you; I am not keen on Willow dating a white man. No offense to you, but I have seen some terrible shit in my lifetime. Lynchings. Cross burnings." He pauses to take a drink. His face hardens as he remembers. "Do you realize that I would have been shot dead for even looking at a white woman?" He asks, not expecting a response. "So, you people really haven't been on my list of favorites."

"I can understand that, sir." I reply.

"Willow is my only child. Her mom and I have busted our asses to make sure that she had a better life, and better opportunities."

"Looks like you guys have done quite well." I say.

He leans forward. "Son, this is where we are today. You have no idea about the struggle it took to get here." He rubs his temple. "But that's another conversation. Back to you and Willow. I want the best for Willow…all around. More importantly, I want the man who ends up with her to honor her in every way. Willow is a good woman. The Mrs. and I have made sure of that, and she deserves a good man. Now, I can't choose who she falls in love with. She always said that she wanted someone like me." He laughs. "Imagine my surprise when she shows up with you. It didn't sit too well, but after talking with you over dinner you seem to have a good head on your shoulders, and you love my daughter. I can see it when you look at her, and she loves you. You're the second man that Willow has introduced me to and that says a lot." Mr. James takes a puff from his cigar and leans towards me, again. "So, I'm gonna' say this to you. Be good to my baby girl…period. Or, as the late Bernie Mac might say, "I'll have to bust your mutha' fuckin' ass." And we wouldn't want that; would we?"

I have to laugh with Mr. James, because I wouldn't hold back shit if it were my child. So, I completely understand.

"No, sir, we wouldn't want that." I reply while chuckling. I take another sip of my scotch and say, "Mr. James, in all seriousness I do love your daughter. I can honestly say that I have never met anyone like Willow. She surprises me every day with something new. I mean, she's witty, smart and of course beautiful; but more than that Mr. James, Willow has a beautiful heart. She is a good person at the core. It's the first time in my life that I feel like a woman truly loves me for me." I feel myself tearing up. "You have my word that I will always honor your daughter, and I have nothing but good intentions when it comes to her. Please know that."

"Alright, son, I'm gonna' hold you to it."

"Please do." I reply.

We talk candidly for another hour or so, while enjoying our cigars and aged scotch. He tells me how he and Mrs. James met. He lights up when he talks about their life together. I want that. I want that with Willow.

CHAPTER 27

Willow and I say goodbye to her parents, and promise to get together again real soon. I open the door for Willow and place my container of carrot cake in the back seat. After fastening my seat belt, I look over at Willow and notice that she's smiling. "What's that big grin for?" I ask.

She doesn't respond. She simply reaches over and places her hand between my legs, and squeezes gently. "Instead of making a left, make a right and go down to the end of this street." She says, while unfastening my belt and unzipping my pants. I am instantly aroused by Willow's grip. My dick begins to pulse. I drive as fast as I can to the end of the street, and Willow motions me to park in a secluded area surrounded with manicured trees. As I park the car, Willow removes her seatbelt. She reaches into the back seat and retrieves the container of carrot cake that her mom gave me. "Here." She hands me the container. "Hold this for a moment." She says matter-of-factly, and she proceeds to pull my dick out of pants. "Open it." She commands. Of course I oblige her request, and open the container. Willow takes two of her fingers and lifts some of the cream cheese frosting off of the cake, and begins to cover my dick with the creamy, sugary mixture. The smooth, cool texture of the cream feels good against my throbbing cock.

Willow removes the container from my hand and places it back in the seat. She then gets on her knees, grabs the base of my dick and begins to lick the cream off, as if it is the most delectable cone she's ever tasted. At first, she uses short, slow licks before engulfing my entire dick inside of her scorching, hot mouth. I tremble as she moves her mouth up and down my shaft, before teasing my balls. I grab her head and she begins this intense suck, while moving my balls up and down with each stroke. This feeling is heavenly.

I grab her ass with my free hand, and begin caressing her. I love the way it feels. It's soft, yet firm. I feel my anxiety getting worse as I slide my hand between Willow's thighs. Even though she's wearing pants, I can feel the wetness of her pussy through the fabric. *Shit, I wanna fuck her.*

My dick is throbbing and I feel myself about to explode. "Wait, baby. Let's wait until we get home." I plead.

"No, Rece, let me take you there, honey. Relax." She says softly.

I recline my seat all the way back and let Willow suck my hard, pounding cock until I explode.

"Yummy, that was nice." She says, before kissing me.

I can taste my cum on her lips. "Yes, it was extremely nice." I reply.

Willow grabs a few wipes from the console and cleans us both off. I snatch another kiss from her before saying, "You know I'm gonna tear that pussy up when we get home."

She replies, "I wouldn't expect anything else…I welcome it."

CHAPTER 28

A few months have passed since we had dinner at my parents' home. We have gotten together a few more times since then, and have had a great time. We even went to church together last Sunday. It was truly a priceless moment to see the faces of the congregation when I walked in with Rece. I expected a few stares, but what I got was beyond a "hot mess". I had sistahs walking up to me saying, "Oh, heyyyyy Willow, girl. I ain't seen you in a while." *She just saw me at the nail salon on Friday.* "Who is this handsome fellow?" They'd ask, while extending their hand and saying, "Ohhhh, God bless you, Rece. Please do visit Mount Olive Christian Center, again. We'd love to have you." They'd purr, while still holding onto his hand. Shit, I know I was in the church, but those so-called sanctified bitches were all over my man, like he was a T-Bone steak, all in the name of Jesus. Don't ever believe that these women are showing up at church dressed like they're going to club, to get the Holy Spirit. They are on a manhunt.

However, the biggest hate came from the brothas. They couldn't even disguise their disdain. I couldn't believe it. As many times as sistahs sit back and watch fine ass brothas scrape the bottom of the barrel when they select a white woman; they can't possibly say shit about Rece.

It's fucked up, and we see it all of the time. Successful black men marrying white women that wouldn't even give them the time of day if it weren't for their money and power…but, a sistah is a gold digger if she wants to date you because you have money. Sistahs have got to be educated, fine, own their own home and car. However, a white girl can step out of a trailer, looking like she's been laying bricks all day, and a brotha will show up at the family barbecue like he's sporting Paris Hilton. At least when sistahs do date outside the race we choose someone decent. So, my thought to all of the hateful stares was simply, "Stare all you want because this white man stepped up to the plate when many of you had the opportunity, but didn't." Don't get me wrong. I love black men. My preference has always been to date, and eventually marry a black man, but that hasn't happened. I've had a few failed relationships with black men, however; it hasn't made me bitter towards brothas. I've just decided to stop limiting myself when it comes to dating. Rece is a wonderful man and he just happens to be white.

After service, my dad and mom introduced Rece to their circle of friends. I could tell that a few of the deacons weren't too thrilled. That's because a few of them have been trying to hit on me behind my dad's back. But, after seeing Daddy's interaction with Rece, they eased up. My parents are quite fond of Rece. Daddy says that he's is a good man, and that he won't hold his whiteness against him. I am really enjoying seeing Rece with my parents. I've only brought one other guy around them; my ex-boyfriend. They weren't too thrilled, but they were cordial. This time things are just flowing.

My doorbell rings. It must be my afternoon client. I walk quickly to the front door and open it. I am in shock. Before I can get a word out…

"Hi, Willow." He says, while flashing his pearly whites, and looking fine as ever. I gotta give it to him. He's fine as fuck, but he ain't worth a dime.

Jordan Michael. He could easily pass for Morris Chestnut, maybe a taller version. He stands about 6'1, and is a beautiful shade of dark chocolate. Not to mention, a body that just won't quit. Jordan is a total fitness freak. He has less than one percent body fat, and makes sure that everyone sees it by wearing the tightest of clothing. And did I mention that he's a good fuck, but he ain't worth shit. Oh, I said that already. He's always gonna do this, or gonna do that…and never really committing to anything. He's started more than six businesses, and has never followed through on any of them. I know for a fact that I gave him over fifty thousand dollars while we were dating. I was trying to be the supportive woman. You know, stand by your man kinda' shit. After a few years, it just got old, and very expensive. Realistically, Jordan just wants someone to take care of him. He thinks like a beautiful woman, with no substance. Do everything for me because I'm beautiful, and I give you a good screw; in the meantime, accept whatever treatment I throw your way. He's a trip. I can't believe I stayed with him as long as I did. What was I thinking?

"Uh, hi, Jordan," I reply completely stunned. "What are you doing here?"

He shifts his feet and puts his hands in his pockets. "Ummm, can we talk?" He asks.

"Well, this really isn't a good time. I'm expecting a client." I say, trying not to sound too firm.

"Hey, it will only take a minute. Please?" He asks, with a sense of sincerity.

"Ok, come on in." I respond as he steps into the foyer. Jordan follows me into my office. "Take a seat," I say, before sitting in my chair. "What's up?"

"Well," he pauses, as he rubs his hands together. "You know" pausing, again. "Willow, are you fucking a white boy?" He asks, with a sense of anger.

I lean forward and clasp my hands. "As a matter-of-fact… I am." I say proudly.

"What?" He asks, as if he didn't believe me. "What did you say?" He asks, again.

"I said, yes. Now what?" Slightly irritated.

"What the fuck, Willow? What kind of bullshit is this?" He yells.

I sit up straight in my chair, "Excuse me? What right do you have showing up at my house to inquire about who I am screwing?"

"I have every right, Willow. I was with you for several years." He says forcefully.

"There's the operative word Jordan…*was* with me. We are no longer together."

Jordan starts pacing the floor. "I can't believe this shit!" He turns towards me. "Do you know how embarrassing it was to hear Devin and my boys talking about this white motherfucker?"

"Embarrassing? Why? We haven't been together for a while now. How does this impact your life?" I ask, with a tone.

"Believe me…it does. I have a reputation to uphold." He says, while stroking his mustache.

Arrogant asshole.

"Ohhh, now we're getting somewhere." I laugh. "It's your reputation you're worried about."

"Shit, yeah. I mean, did I mess you up so bad that you have given up on brothers? If that's the case, I'll take you back because I don't want you suffering like this." He sits down again, but this time on the edge of his seat.

I can't contain it, this is too funny. I mean the nerve of this man. "Wow, this is amazing." I smile, as I get up and sit next to Jordan. I take a moment to gather my composure, because I'm trying desperately not to die from laughter. "Jordan, when I was with you. I loved you…sincerely. There's nothing that I wouldn't have done for you, but that was long ago. I mean, I am sooo over you. You're a chapter that's been closed for a quite some time. For you to think that you somehow play a role in who I choose to be with is utterly ridiculous." I can't hold it anymore. I laugh until my stomach starts hurting. This of course pisses Jordan off.

"What the fuck are you laughing about? This shit isn't funny!" He shouts.

"You don't think so?" I ask while leaning back in my chair.

"Hell no!"

"Oh well, you'll get over it." I stand to indicate that this conversation is about to come to an end.

"Well, I know your parents don't like this shit. Your dad would flip out if you showed up with a white boy." He says with confidence.

I smile. "To be perfectly honest with you, my parents really like him. Rece and Dad have even golfed a few times. Oh, I forgot, you never got invited to golf with Dad did you?" Smirking.

Jordan stands, and replies sharply, "I don't believe that shit."

"Believe it." I say with an edge. "Now, if there's nothing else, I'm going to ask you to leave."

"This is fucked up, Willow!" Jordan yells while walking towards the front door. When he reaches the front door, he turns towards me and runs his hand down my arm. "Seriously though, Willow, I miss that." He licks his lips. I reach for the handle and open the door. "Ahhh, that's how you gonna do a brotha?" Throwing his hands up. "Ohhh, you too good for me now that you got a white boy?" He asks, while stepping onto the porch.

I give him a serious stare and reply, "Actually, I was too good for you back then. I just didn't know better. Now, have a blessed day." I close the door, but not before hearing him say, "Bitch! That's why I left yo' ass!"

Wow! Did he say he left me? He must be delusional.

CHAPTER 29

Whew! I am finally finished with my afternoon client, and decide to call Journey to tell her about my visitor. The phone rings three times before she answers. "Hello, this is Journey."

"Hey girl, it's me."

"Hey, Willow. What's happening? I was just about to call you to see if you and Rece wanted to have dinner with us tonight." She rolls off quickly.

"That would be great. I really don't feel like cooking, tonight, but I know that Rece will be hungry when he gets off. This new subdivision has been kicking his ass."

"Why?" Journey asks. "Doesn't he have people to do all of the building and stuff?"

I laugh. "Yes, Journey, he does have a crew, but Rece likes to do a lot of the work himself. Especially when it comes to his custom homes." I explain.

"Girrrrrrl, if you and Rece get married you are gonna have a house out of this world!" She exclaims, with a chuckle. "Shit, you gonna have all that imported stuff. I can't wait."

"Aren't you a little ahead of yourself? I mean, Rece hasn't exactly popped the question." I reply.

"Chile, it's just a matter of time. As much time as the two of you are spending together, and your parents like him…ohhh, I'd bet my last dime that it will be real soon." She laughs. "You know you love that white boy!"

"Journey, you are crazy. I do love Rece, but I don't want to get ahead of myself. I'll cross that bridge when I get to it."

"Whatever, bitch!"

We both laugh.

"You almost made me forget why I was calling your black ass." Pausing to stop myself from laughing. "Guess who showed up at my door today?"

"Who?" Journey asks, inquisitively.

"Jordan." I reply.

"What the fuck, Willow?" Journey screams through the phone. "Get outta here!"

"Yeah, I know." I reply in agreement.

"What did he want?"

"Girl, he had the audacity to come over here, and question me about whether or not I was dating a white man." I say, with a bit of anger.

"Shut up, Willow! You have got to be kidding me?" She replies in shock.

"No, Journey. I am serious. He said that Devin and his boys were talking about his ex dating a white boy, and he has a reputation to uphold."

Journey can't hold her laughter. "A reputation to uphold? Is he serious?"

"Yeah, girl. He was all in my face and then get this, I basically try to tell him that I am dating someone that happens to be white, and that he should just stay out of my business. Well, we get to the front door and he tries to push up on me by saying he really misses it." I crack up just thinking about it, again. Journey is cracking up, too.

"No, he didn't." Journey snaps.

"I couldn't believe it, but that's not everything. When he sees that I don't give a fuck and was closing the door on his ass; he says, "That's why I left yo' ass…bitch!"

"Nooo, that muthafucka didn't." Journey says, angrily.

"Yes, he did." I respond.

"Girl, he is just jealous. I bet Devin and his boys wore his sorry ass out. They were all over here the other night, just chillin', and I overheard them saying that Jordan fucked up and that you were a good woman. Then someone else said that he should feel like shit handing you over to a white boy. And you know my nosey ass chimed in, uninvited, into the conversation." She laughs.

"I told them that Jordan didn't hand you over to nobody; you simply walked away from his, "Give me some time baby to get myself together, to I'm gonna open up this sports bar, to I'm gonna build ponds for rich people in Green Hills, to I think I want to open a car wash, to I'm gonna go back to school to get my M.B.A, to I need to borrow another $10,000 to start this real estate thing, to I know I haven't called you in two weeks but I was tied up, to damn the white man always tryin to keep a brotha down"—to you snapping out of a freaking fog and saying—"Fuck you, Jordan, I'm out!" Girl, they hit the floor laughing. Devin told me to get my ass back in the bedroom, and stay out of their conversation. Shiiit, I didn't care because they knew I was right."

I can't stop laughing. My girl, Journey, is too much. "Journey, you are a mess, but you are my fucking girl, and you ain't told nothing but the truth. You know that I gave my all to Jordan, and he was just trifling with a capital T."

"Well, honey, that is water way under the bridge. As my grandma says, "If God intended for you to live in the past he would have put eyes on the back of your head."

We both laugh in unison. "I know that's right. Thanks for having my back, Journey."

"Always Willow…always." She replied, lovingly.

We talk for another hour and decide to meet at Chappy's on Church Street at seven. I'm looking forward to a pleasant evening.

CHAPTER 30

We pull up in front of Chappy's a little after seven. I see Journey and Devin about to walk inside of the restaurant. The valet opens the passenger door for Rece, and then walks around to the driver's side of my car and opens the door for me. I swing both of my legs out of the car, making sure to keep my knees together, as not to reveal my naked bottom. Yet, I catch the valet checking out my mocha thighs. I smile and decide to just let him enjoy the view, and not embarrass him for taking a glance. He quickly hands me my ticket and I walk towards Rece, who extends his hand to help me onto the sidewalk. I love holding hands with Rece. It's as if our hands were made for each other. I smile at the thought.

There is an older, distinguished looking gentleman holding the door for us as we enter the restaurant. He greets us with a strong, southern accent, "Good evening, and welcome to Chappy's."

"Thank you." We both reply.

Once inside, we immediately see Journey waving us toward our table. Chappy's is a wonderful restaurant that specializes in New Orleans cuisine. I love eating here, because the atmosphere is so cozy and they always have great live jazz.

Rece and I make it to our table, and he and Devin greet each other and shake hands, while Journey and I give each other our usual hug and kiss. Rece pulls my chair out, and then takes a seat beside me.

"Mmmm, it smells good in here." Journey says.

"I know, it does." I say, while taking a long whiff of the aromas floating in the air. "Plus, I am starving."

An attractive waitress approaches our table and offers us menus, while giving us a detailed description of each special being offered. The waitress is tall, about 5'10", chocolate brown, with a fly-ass bob, and kind of on the thick side. She's cute. I like that she's personable, but not over the top. She recognizes our fine men, but doesn't flirt. Journey and I will make sure that she gets a big tip for the respect. She tells us that her name is Brittany, and that she'll give us a few minutes to look over the menus. Just then, another server comes to the table and pours us each a glass of water.

"Other than water, would you like anything else to drink?" Brittany kindly asks.

"Ummm, how about a bottle of your Chardonnay?" Devin replies.

"The Patz & Hall, or the Talbott?" Brittany asks.

"Both are excellent choices. How about the Patz & Hall?"

"Excellent choice, sir. Someone will be right out with your wine." Brittany smiles, and quickly walks off. Journey nudges Devin and says, "You can look. Don't be acting like she ain't cute." Journey bursts into laughter.

"Man, ain't nobody checking out the waitress. Chill." Devin takes a sip of water.

Journey leans towards Devin. "Are you trying to tell me that you didn't notice that Brittany was cute?"

"I'm not trying to tell you anything, Journey. Stop tripping." Devin sighs.

"Journey, why are you tripping? The waitress is cute. So what?" I ask, while chuckling.

"Girrrrl, I'm just messing with him. He always tries to act like he doesn't look, but I know he does." Journey says with a smirk, and then kisses Devin on the cheek.

"You are a trip." Devin says, before cracking a smile. He knows that my girl can be a little psycho at times. He turns his eyes towards Rece and says, "Rece, man it's good to see you again. What have you been up to?"

"Ahhh, not a whole lot. Just working, and trying to keep this lady smiling." Rece reaches for my hand, and I instantly blush.

Devin leans back slightly in his chair and says, "Shoot, I feel for you." Devin laughs.

Journey chimes in, "Me, too, 'cause my girl ain't no joke!"

I chuckle in disbelief. "I know you are not going there, Miss I'm Gonna Drill My Man About The Waitress". Everyone dies laughing. "Forget both of you." I say. "My baby isn't hurting for anything. Are you, baby?"

Rece leans towards me and plants a gentle kiss on my lips. "Not a thing," he whispers.

"Oh please, you two love birds. Give us a break." Journey jokes.

Rece and Devin return to their conversation, while Journey and I chit chat. "As I was saying, Devin, things are good."

"That's good, dawg. I thought I saw one of your construction signs on Jefferson Street the other day."

"Yeah, we're getting ready to break ground on some new row houses. The entire Jefferson Street area is about to be huge."

"Really?" Devin inquires, with a tone of seriousness.

"Seriously. You should really look into doing something over there." Rece says before taking a sip of his water.

"Well, to be perfectly honest with you, I've always been interested in construction and development, but have never had the opportunity to really delve into it." Devin responds.

"I tell you what. Come by my office next Saturday, and I'll take you around to some of our projects and give you the inside scoop on some things. Afterwards, if you are really serious about this business, I'll be more than happy to assist you. Deal?"

"Deal!" Devin and Rece give each other dap. "Man, that's really cool of you to extend yourself like this." Devin says.

"It's nothing, man. I'm in a place to do it. My dad built this business from the ground up, and put our family in a really good place. It's only right that I share. Plus, you're a good guy."

"Well, I appreciate it, and I will be there next Saturday." I am happy that Rece and Devin like each other. I was a little worried with Rece being white, and Devin being best friends with my ex, but things have worked out just fine. It's a good thing.

We all notice Brittany walking back to our table, and quickly try to make our selections from the menu.

"Has everyone decided what they want to eat?" She asks with a smile.

"Yes." Devin answers. "We'd like to start off with the gumbo and fried green tomatoes. Then, I think I'll have the Veal Alexander."

"Ditto." Rece interjects.

"Devin glances towards Journey, and she says, "You already know what I want. The trout almondine."

"She'll have the trout." Pausing slightly. "What about you, Willow?"

"I think I'll have the trout, too. Yeah, that'll work."

"Okay, then. The veal and trout it is."

We all nod in unison. "Excellent choices!" Brittany says, and then let's us know that the wine will be out shortly. A few seconds later a gentleman arrives at our table with the bottle of Chardonnay. He offers the first taste to Devin. Devin extends the glass a few inches, looks at the color, and gently swirls the liquid before allowing his nose to take in all of the delicate aromas. He takes a sip and smiles at the waiter to indicate his pleasure. The waiter takes his cue, and fills each of our glasses. We lift our glasses and I say, "To friendship!"

Everyone repeats, "To friendship!"

Just when we're all about to take a sip from our wine glasses, Journey clears her throat and says, "I don't believe this shit! No this muthafucka didn't!" She exclaims before slamming her glass on the table. We all follow her glaring stare towards the front door, and see Jordan hugged up with some Pamela Anderson wannabe, sporting 52DDD boobs. Oh my, I'm not hating, but she looks a hot mess. I am sure that Macy's could re-stock every makeup counter in their store with the products on her face. And to top it all, if she were to sneeze, you could see all of her business. Basically, she's wearing a thin strip of spandex. Wow! This is really too much to take in all at once. She is definitely the prototype of plastic surgery gone way wrong.

Of course Jordan sees us and starts to make his way towards where we are sitting. I don't know if I can take him twice in one day.

Journey turns to Devin and asks, "Did you tell him that we were coming here tonight?"

"Yeah, but I didn't think he would show up. Damn, this ain't cool. Ain't cool at all." Devin shakes head.

I glance over at Rece and he replies, "Naw man, actually it is cool…ice water cool."

I reach under the table, and place my hand on Rece's knee. I have a feeling that this isn't going to end on a pleasant note.

CHAPTER 31

Jordan makes his way over to our table, while wearing his usual Cheshire cat grin. Blond girl is holding onto his arm as if she has landed Tiger Woods. Journey gives me a look that says, "If she only knew. She'd drop that Negro like a hot potato."

"Well…" dragging the word out in a cynical manner, "…hello, people. Fancy seeing all of you here this evening." He laughs up under his breath, as if there's something humorous in all of this. Maybe there is, I'm just not feeling it right now.

"Man, what are you doing?" Devin asks, with a disgusted look.

"What?" Jordan replies dumbfounded. "Can't a brotha have a nice quiet dinner with a special friend?" He puts emphasis on the word special, as if to invoke some type of response from me. I laugh to myself at his level of ignorance.

"Whatever, dude! This is sooooo childish." Devin firmly states, before taking a sip of wine.

Blond girl clears her throat, and Jordan gets the obvious hint. "Oh, everyone this is Tiffany." He flashes a huge smile in my direction.

We all say in unison, "Hello, Tiffany."

She greets us with an over the top Valley Girl voice, that instantly drives us crazy and we quickly tune her out. Meanwhile, Jordan extends his hand to Rece. "Ahhh, you must be Rece. Willow's new man?"

Rece shakes his hand and replies, "That I am."

Laughing. "I see you got a little Jungle Fever, too!" Jordan tries to give Rece dap. Rece doesn't respond. Jordan continues making a fool out of himself. "Yeah, I decided to give this vanilla honey a try, since chocolate is so outdated. You see, I've had chocolate just about every way you can have it. Plain. With whip cream. With a few sprinkles. Hot chocolate. Cold chocolate. Luke warm chocolate." Jordan sticks his chest out slightly, and pats it.

Rece laughs, leans back and says, "Wow man, jealousy is a female trait."

Jordan steps back slightly. "What? What the fuck? White boy you tryin' to spew some Jay-Z on a brotha?" Jordan says, before letting go of his date's hand. Rece hasn't moved. He doesn't raise his voice, or lose his composure, but replies, "Oh, you know about Jay- Z? 'Cause from your bitch-ass behavior I can't tell." Rece stands.

"Ooooh, I guess you weren't expecting that, were you?" Journey snaps. Devin immediately gives her that look that says, "Shut the fuck up!" She knows the look, and quickly calms down.

Jordan is infuriated with Rece's response. He walks up to Rece, points his finger in his face and says, "Man, I will fuck your white-ass up!"

Rece shifts his weight slightly and replies, "Listen here, don't let the white fool you. I'm the only muthafucka' that will be doing the fucking. Now get your punk-ass finger out of my face."

"Hell naw!" Jordan yells, before throwing a punch at Rece's face. Luckily, Rece blocks his punch and quickly throws some Bruce Lee karate move, hitting Jordan in the throat. Jordan tumbles to the floor screaming that he can't breathe. At that point, we all stand up as two security guards quickly approach our table. Of course everyone in the restaurant is in full gear watching this play out. I must admit, we were all a bit concerned when Jordan said he couldn't breathe, even though he started all of this mess. "He'll be ok." Rece says. "Just a really sore throat for the next few days."

Tiffany leans over Jordan as if he were a sick puppy. "Ahhh, baby. Are you okay? Officer arrest this man. He hit my boyfriend!"

"Well, young lady, from where we were standing, it looked as if your boyfriend here just bit off more than he could chew." The security guard says, in a strong southern accent. "Now, why don't you and your boyfriend head on home, and call it a night. I don't think these lovely folks want to press any charges."

The other guard helps Jordan to his feet, and he slowly walks out of the restaurant with his tail between his legs. I look at Rece and apologize.

"You don't have anything to apologize for." He says, while grabbing my hand.

"You sure in the hell don't! You can't help it if your ex is a loser!" Journey says, before making a motion to zip her lips. We all laugh. My girl is a trip.

Devin is still in shock. "I cannot believe my boy. This is some crazy shit." Devin throws his hands up in the air. "I can't call it. Let's just enjoy the rest of our evening."

"I hear ya. Where were we before the drama?" Rece asks with a smile.

Once again, we lift our glasses and toast. I let out a long sigh of relief. *Please God, no more drama.*

CHAPTER 32

Thanksgiving is just around the corner, and Willow will officially meet my parents. I am praying that the meeting will go over successfully. Of course, my brother and his wife adore Willow, and I'm sure my dad will love her, too, but I can't say the same for my mom. She doesn't mean any harm, but she's never really dealt with her hurt regarding Dad messing around with black women.

She thinks that Bronson and I are clueless about my father's infidelity. Truth be told, we've known practically all of our lives. It's common conversation around my dad, uncles and their friends.

I've never liked the fact that Dad cheats on Mom, but I also don't like how Mom has never made Dad accountable. Love means being accountable to each other. I could never treat Willow the way Dad treats Mom. It's actually quite tragic.

I can already hear my dad, "Damn, son, you did good! I guess you got your good taste from me." He'll laugh, and unharmingly, flirt with Willow. He will believe that he had some influence in me selecting Willow. How wrong he will be.

Mom, however, will hit the roof. Hopefully, it won't last for more than five minutes. I've already prepared Willow. She laughed and said that it couldn't be any worse than my first meeting with her dad. Man, she has no clue.

I have also made an important decision about my life. I want to marry Willow. She is the one. I have no doubt that this is the woman I want to spend the rest of my life with. She's everything that I have prayed for and more.

My brother told me that it would happen like this. True love that is. He said that when I finally met "the one" I'd start visualizing her not just as a mate, but as a mother. And if I could only see her as a wife, and not a mother,…she's not the one. Meaning, she's fine as fuck, but doesn't have a drop of maternal instinct running through her veins. Bronson is a trip, but he is dead on with this.

Willow is undoubtedly the best woman I have come across. I can see us having a beautiful life together, with a house full of children. Well, maybe two or three, because Willow isn't trying to mess up her figure. I think she'll be a great mom.

Initially, I was going to propose to Willow while we were in Italy. We just returned home after spending a week in Florence. We chose Florence because we both love art, architecture, and of course wine. We brought back some amazing Tuscan wines. I can't wait to open a bottle. Plus, after the momentary drama with Willow's ex, we needed to get away. He kept calling her for about a month or so after the incident, and then stopped. We really thought that she would have to pursue a restraining order, but luckily it didn't get that far. It's hard for a man to lose. Especially when he knows that he had the opportunity to come out on the winning end, had he paid attention and cherished what he had. Oh well, one man's trash is another man's treasure. I'm glad he didn't recognize what he had. Shit, I'm downright ecstatic.

Since I knew I wanted to propose to Willow, I decided to do this on a more formal level. I'm going to ask her dad and mom for her hand, rather than just ask her alone. I think that she and her parents will appreciate the consideration. Not to mention, Willow's dad means the world to her and she wouldn't want him overlooked on this special moment in her life. I met with our family jeweler before I left for Italy, and he should have Willow's ring ready today. So, I'm going stop by his shop, swing by the cigar bar in Mount Juliet, and then meet with Mr. and Mrs. Williams.

Damn, I'm nervous as hell. Oh well, its do or die! I told my brother that I was going to propose and he was really happy. I think he's just tired of being the "married" brother. It will be nice seeing Mindy and Willow planning family gatherings and our children growing up together. I can't wait. Life is good.

CHAPTER 33

"Sooo, Oliver, it's been a few months since the divorce, huh? How are you holding up?" I ask, with a sense of tenderness, while sitting up a little straighter in my chair.

"Well, not so good." He rubs his hands together, while looking out of the window. "I miss her a lot."

"That's normal, but how are you in terms of getting back to normal?"

He turns towards me, and then lowers his mahogany eyes. I know the answer before he opens his mouth. "You mean, have I gotten rid of all of her stuff?"

"Precisely." I state firmly.

Oliver stands and starts pacing the room. He puts his hands in his pockets, and stops in the middle of my Persian rug and just stares at it for a while. I don't say anything, because I really want him to talk. So, I simply sit and wait for his response.

"Nah, not yet," he fidgets, "I guess a part of me thinks that she'll come back." I notice a small tear cascading down his caramel, chiseled face. "But, that's not gonna happen, huh?" He asks, with a type of tone that's expecting a positive response.

I reply, "In all probability, no. She's not coming back, but it's not the end of the world. You still have a lot more living to do. You're a successful, black man. Believe me, you will not have any problems finding love, again." I chuckle, hoping to get a smile, but instead he remains stoic. So, I stand and walk towards him.

"Oliver, I know this hurts, but eventually the pain will go away. It's gonna take one day at a time, but in the meantime, I need for you to get rid of her things and any reminders that prevent you from progressing. Okay?"

"Yeah, okay." He says unconvincingly.

I grab his hands, and look him directly in the eyes. "Call Goodwill and have them come and remove all of her stuff. The sooner you get this done, the sooner you will be on your way towards some peace and happiness. It's time to heal."

"I know, I know. I still can't believe that Staci left me for my brother. How low can a person get?" Oliver sits back down, and begins tapping his foot nervously. I walk back to my seat and remove my glasses.

"It's a tragic situation for both families involved. No one won. The only positive aspect is that there were no children involved. So, the only person that you have to concentrate on right now is you." I say.

"Yeah, you've got a point there." He agrees and stands. That's my indication that he's tired of talking. At least for now.

"Alright, Oliver. This has been a good session. I'll see you next month?"

"Yes…yes, you will." He finally smiles.

"Take care of yourself." I say, while trying to contain my sadness.

Oliver waves goodbye and walks out.

"Whew! That was hard." I lean back in my chair to get my composure. God, I feel so bad for him.

Oliver Thompson is my attorney, my friend and most recently, my client. He is such a great guy. Smart, good looking, generous...the complete package. Several years ago, he left one of the biggest law firms in Nashville, and opened his own firm in the heart of the black community on Jefferson Street. His younger brother joined his practice shortly thereafter. Business was booming. Oliver and his wife, Staci, were Nashville's premiere black, power couple. They were known for throwing the best social parties in town. They spared no expense when it came to entertaining. It wasn't unusual to attend one of their parties and leave with some designer party favor, especially designed for the event. They have been known to give away Gucci wallets, Louis Vuitton sunglasses, the list goes on and on. Then it happened. Everything came tumbling down.

I had no idea what was going on when Oliver called me from jail. He was hysterical. It took several minutes before I could make any sense of what he was trying to tell me.

He had to leave town for a few days to wrap up a case he had in Atlanta. Initially, his younger brother, Darren, was to accompany him, but cancelled at the last minute. He said that he needed to secure a new client. So, Oliver went to Atlanta, alone. He ended up finishing in three days, rather than four, and returned home early. Instead of going straight home, he dropped off some files at his firm, picked up some fresh flowers to surprise Staci, and headed home.

When he arrived at his house, he noticed several cars parked out front. He figured Staci was throwing another "Girl's Day Out" luncheon with her girlfriends. Oliver found a parking space, grabbed the flowers and headed towards his front door. He could hear the music blasting before he entered. He thought Staci and her girlfriends were truly enjoying themselves.

When he opened his front door he could not believe his eyes. There had to be twenty naked couples in his living room, screwing like rabbits. He quickly spotted his wife being fucked by none other than his brother, while she sucked the dick of one of the most powerful white judges in Nashville. Needless to say, he put a whooping on everything in sight, including his wife. It was a mess. Several top dignitaries were participating in this group orgy. The media had a field day. Oliver was devastated.

I posted his bail, and literally watched a grown man drown in his sorrows for five days. It was by far the saddest thing I've ever witnessed.

Staci and Darren refused to press charges, along with everyone else that was involved. Staci wrote him a "Dear John" letter and left town with his brother. Thus, began our therapy sessions.

Once he got through the initial shock of everything, he started coming around; but you can still see his hurt. Losing your wife is one thing, but losing her to your baby brother, is a whole different ball game. I'm hoping that our sessions will help him heal quicker. I suggested that he talk to a therapist that specialized in divorce, but he said that he felt more comfortable with me. Plus, he didn't want his business all over Nashville.

I think he'll be okay. It's just going to take some time.

Speaking of time, it's getting late. I have an afternoon manicure and pedicure scheduled. Rece says that we're going on a "hot" date day after tomorrow. I can't wait!

I'm still basking in the glow of Italy. Our trip was more than fabulous, it was absolutely splendid. Everything was perfect. The food, the wine, the site seeing and of course, the sex. Lord Jesus, this man puts it *DOWN*.

It had been a while since I traveled to Italy. I can still remember my very first trip. I was ten-years old, and fascinated about seeing Lorenzo Ghiberti's famous bronze doors.

My parents started taking me to the library at a very early age. Each week we drove to the Hadley Park Library near Tennessee State University and they let me select three books. Then they chose one book for me to read and to give them a full, verbal report. One day, they handed me a book simply titled *Italy,* and thus began my fascination.

I became engrossed in everything, from the art of Leonardo da Vinci, to the carvings of Donatello. When I saw photos of the bronze doors, I begged my parents to take me to Italy for our annual summer vacation. The school year ended in May, and we boarded a plane the first week of June. I was the happiest kid in America, and Italy became my special place.

Being able to experience it with Rece puts the icing on the cake. You always hear about how romantic Italy can be, but you never really know until you visit it with the one you love.

CHAPTER 34

It's a little past noon, and I'm leaving the smoke shop in Mount Juliet, and heading to Stoney River to meet Mr. and Mrs. James. My stomach has been nervous all morning. It's not that I'm scared about asking the James' for their daughter's hand, it's just the magnitude of what this decision means for me.

Marriage…wow, this is huge! I suppose like most men, I have thought about marriage, but only in a vague, futuristic kind of way. It wasn't until I met Willow that I actually saw myself in the role of a husband.

It's truly amazing how a good woman can completely turn your life around. Because to be completely honest, I was just running through women. It was all empty and meaningless…just sex. There have been a few times when I thought, "Maybe this could be the one," but after a few dates, I always had my answer. They all just wanted the name and status.

However, when real love takes hold of your heart, it truly changes everything. It makes you want to do right. It's a beautiful thing.

I maneuver through the afternoon traffic on West End Avenue, and laugh at all of the business people in their

Eddie Bauer and Jones of New York attire. I also notice the casually dressed students from Vanderbilt University, in baggy cargo shorts, graphic tees and Keds, all texting while walking. Oblivious to anyone or anything around them. When did cell phones become such a fixed item in our lives? *Who knows.*

I pull into the parking lot of Stoney River and valet. Realizing that I don't have any cash on me to tip the drivers, I quickly dash next door to the bank to withdraw some money. As I'm walking back, I see Mr. and Mrs. James pulling up to the restaurant in a deep, granite-colored Bentley Azure. It's a beautifully crafted vehicle. The James have superb taste. I stand at the entrance and wait while they valet. Mr. James gently takes Mrs. James by the hand as they walk towards me. I take a few steps and shake his hand.

"Hello, sir. It's a pleasure to see you, again." I say.

"Likewise, son. How are you?" He asks with a smile.

"Actually, I'm great, sir. Things couldn't be better!" I say, with slight excitement.

"My kinda boy!" Mr. James pats me on the back.

I lean towards Mrs. James and kiss her on the cheek. "You look beautiful as always, ma'am."

She blushes before saying, "I do believe we'll keep you around, if only for the compliments."

We both laugh.

"I'll take whatever I can get ma'am." I reply. I quickly grab the door and we head inside. We are greeted by two very attractive hostesses. Both young ladies are a perfect size four, with equal perfectly-shaped 38DD fake boobs. Neither has seemed to go too far with Botox injections, so they are still pretty. They both smile and subtly flirt. I smile back, not because I'm interested, but I know that a smile will get us seated immediately. I'm positive that they are under the impression that I am about to conduct a business meeting with this African American couple, since this happens to be one of the lunch meeting "hot spots" in Nashville. Little do they know that I am lunching with my soon to be in-laws.

I chuckle at how amazed they would be if they knew. I am positive that their flirtatious behavior would cease immediately, and the temperature in the restaurant would fall below freezing. *I won't spoil their fun.*

We are quickly seated in a comfortable, leather-backed booth, with a small, intimate candle. A pleasant-looking waiter, who looks identical to the lead singer in Maroon 5, introduces himself and takes our orders. A bubbly, redhead appears shortly thereafter with a small platter of sweet rolls and honey butter. Mrs. James takes one of the rolls, splits it half, butters one side and offers it to Mr. James. He quickly devours the sweet, hot delight. I smile at how they interact.

Our waiter returns with a bottle of Greg Norman Shiraz. He offers the first taste to me before filling the remaining glasses.

"Let's toast!" Mr. James says cheerfully, while grabbing his glass.

"What shall we toast to, darling?" Mrs. James asks.

"To love and family." He says.

We all lift our glasses in unison and repeat, "To love and family." We gently tap our glasses. I take a long sip of the Shiraz, and allow the hints of blackberry and cedar to linger in my mouth for a moment before swallowing. After a deep breath, I clear my throat and lean forward, while clinching my glass, unconsciously.

"Mr. and Mrs. James," they both direct their eyes towards me, "let me start off by saying thank you for having lunch with me, today."

"Anytime son." Mrs. James replies.

"Well," pausing slightly to give my heart a chance to stop beating so fast, "I'm not very good at beating around the bush, so I will get straight to the point." I remove my hands from my glass and clasp them together. I take another deep breath. *Come on, Rece, it's do or die, buddy.* "I love, Willow! I mean, I really love her. Not in a superficial, fly-by-night way but, I love the essence of Willow. I love how she laughs. I love how her forehead wrinkles when she's in deep thought. I love her imitation of Tammy Wynette." They both laugh. "I love how she cares for me. Your daughter is the most genuine soul I have ever met, and I honestly don't want to go a day without her in my life." I notice Mr. James shift in his seat. "So, I came here today to ask you for your daughter's hand in marriage."

I reach into my jacket and pull out a small, black velvet box. I open it and place it in the center of the table. Sitting inside the box is a stunning ten- carat cushion diamond. The stone is surrounded by a beautiful, custom diamond and platinum band.

Mrs. James gasps. "Rece, it is absolutely beautiful!" She picks up the box, smiles and passes it to her husband. Mr. James pulls out his glasses and examines the diamond before placing it back on the table. He looks me square in the face and says, "This is my baby Rece, my baby girl."

"I know, sir." I say with compassion. I know what he isn't saying. The love he has for his daughter can't be put into words. He'll lay his life down for her. So, to hand that over to another man is huge.

"You did good, son." He smiles, and then looks at his wife before saying, "We'd be honored to have you as a son." He stands, and I slide out of the booth and stand in front of him. He embraces me hard and whispers in my ear, "Take care of my baby, Rece. Promise me you'll always take care of her?"

"I promise, sir. I promise."

He steps back, looks at me and says, 'Cuz if you don't…"

"You'll have to bust my white ass!"

We laugh a hearty laugh. I think we both saw visions of the first night we met.

Mrs. James stands and gives me a hug. "Willow did good, too!"

"Thank you." I reply, before helping her back into the booth. We sit down just in time. Our food has arrived. Mrs. James blesses the food and we continue talking about my plans to propose to Willow, and them meeting my family at Thanksgiving dinner. They say that they are excited.

"Thanksgiving will be perfect. We will have so much to be thankful for." Mrs. James says happily. Mr. James nods in agreement.

"Son, when are you planning on popping the question?" He asks.

"I plan on asking her tomorrow evening. I have something really special in mind." I find myself blushing at the thought.

Mrs. James chimes in, "Well, I am positive that she will be the happiest camper in Nashville after tomorrow evening. I can't wait to see her afterwards. She deserves it. She's a good woman, if I must say so myself." Glowing as she talks about her only child.

I smile. "That she is." I say, before diving into my meal.

Chapter 35

"Whew! What a day!" I exclaim, before turning my computer off and forwarding my office phones to voicemail. I reach behind my head and remove the hair pins from my bun. They have been annoying me all day, but I really didn't feel like dealing with my hair today. So, I opted out for the ever faithful bun. Quick, easy and professional.

I glance at the clock on my desk, and slowly begin to massage my scalp before leaning back into my chair. While taking a deep breath in, I allow my body to relax. I close my eyes and replay some of today's sessions. They have been interesting to say the least.

My clients seem to be getting more and more complex. I mean shit, I set out to help individuals get on track and achieve their goals. I had no idea that I would become the Dr. Phil of Nashville. I'm not a psychologist. I'm a life coach for crying out loud. I was just telling Journey and Rece that I needed to change my marketing because I am attracting far too many people that need psychological assistance, rather than life coaching skills. It's becoming overwhelming. Rece suggested that I bring in a partner...possibly a therapist. That way, when someone becomes a client, they are working on their entire being. It sounded good in theory, but I do truly enjoy working alone. The only person that I could possibly see myself sharing an office with is Journey.

I think I am just going to scale my client list back, and work with a new marketing firm to attract the type of people that *The Right Path* desires.

Like today, one of my clients comes in totally stressed. I could tell that she was stressed because she always smokes when she is stressed, and I immediately smelled the cigarettes on her when she entered. Kimber Livingston owns one of the hippest, unisex salons in Nashville. *His Style---Her Style Salon and Spa* has a reputation for housing some of the best stylists in Nashville. The great thing about the salon is that she has hair stylists and makeup artists that can do hair for every ethnic group under the sun. Her stylists come from all over the world, and they charge a pretty penny for their work. So, if you're African American sporting a natural 'fro, or an Asian chick that desperately wants curly hair; Kimber's salon has got you covered. Plus, she also has a tanning salon. This chick is racking in the dough.

Kimber is an okay looking white girl, not pretty, maybe a five. She has a really nice figure (built like a sistah), and is always together from head to toe. Kimber wears her hair short and dyed a deep burgundy, with striking blonde streaks. Only she could pull this look off. However, when you factor in that she's rich, that bumps her up to a seven or eight, in the eyes of most men.

Kimber walked in wearing a bad ass Tom Ford, winter white pantsuit, with a dainty, black chiffon blouse underneath. The sheerness of the blouse wasn't overpowering, but added just the right amount of sexiness to the strong, power suit. I have to give it to her; Kimber has great taste.

"Gurrrrl, I am so happy to see you." She says in her most ethnic tone, before plopping down on my sofa. She crosses her legs and gives me a huge smile, while looking around my office, as if she's never stepped foot in here before. She's a trip. I really want to tell her that I detest when white girls or anyone for that matter feels the need to "talk black" when they are dealing with African Americans. It's as if they are trying to say, "Yeah, I'm down." When in fact it's the most *un*-down thing they could ever do. It's especially bad with white girls like Kimber, because she's married to a black guy and she is constantly trying to validate herself around other blacks. She goes over the top trying to prove that she's not like other white women.

For instance, every time that she comes to an appointment she is insistent on discussing the reality shows *Love & Hip Hop* or *Basketball Wives of Miami*. I don't know how many times I have told her that I do not watch that crap. I have seen enough of black women making fools out of themselves on television. I am not adding one iota to the ratings of these ridiculous shows. But, I allow her to talk about whatever she chooses for the first few minutes of our session.

"Girlfriend, I think she was sleeping with her man, because she is a known slut in Miami. I wouldn't put it past her. That bitch better watch out!" She laughs out loud, before opening her purse and pulling out her cigarette case. I give her a stern look and she says, "Uhhh, I forgot. No smoking in the office. My bad."

I open her file and browse through the notes from our last session and respond, "No problem. Enough of the reality shows. How are you?" I emphasize *you*.

"Oh, I'm okay. I'm good." She re-crosses her legs, as I give her the "I don't believe you" look.

Tapping my pen lightly and leaning forward I ask, "Soooo, what have you decided?"

Looking rather dumbfounded. "About what?" Kimber asks.

Is she out of her mind? Just last week she said that she walked into her salon and caught one of her male stylists giving her husband a blow job. And she's really asking me about what? Wow!

"Well, last week you were pretty upset after catching Mike with your stylist."

"Oh, that." She says nonchalantly.

"Yes, that." I respond, matter-of-factly.

She sits frozen, with a blank stare across her face. It's as if she is replaying the scene in her mind. I see the sadness in her eyes, but she quickly snaps out of the thought and lets out a hearty laugh. "Oh, that. It was nothing. I really overreacted." She shifts in her seat, again.

After hearing this, I decide that I better sit up straight to make sure that I am hearing correctly. "You overreacted?" I ask, with dismay and concern.

"Yeah, Mike said that it was just a joke."

"A joke?" I ask, with a higher level of volume and tone.

Kimber begins to talk, but I immediately notice that she isn't looking me directly in the eye. "See, Mike and Ben (the stylist) made a bet that Ben couldn't give a better blow job than me. So, he let him suck his dick to find out," pausing for a moment, "I guess, he was curious. Some men are like that, you know."

Rubbing my brow, "And, you're okay with this?" I ask, quite puzzled.

"Yeah, I'm cool. It's not like Mike is gay or anything." She says, sort of like a question and answer all in one.

Are you out of your fucking mind? No straight man allows another man to suck his dick out of curiosity. PERIOD!

I am trying desperately to keep my composure. "Kimber, darling…" I pause for a moment to take a sip from my bottled water. "can you honestly sit here and say that you have no problem with another man performing oral sex on your husband for a bet, or any other reason for that matter?"

"Nah. I'm not saying that. I'm just saying that it isn't that big a deal. Now, if Mike was gay, then I'd be worried. But, he was just having fun." She says with a straight face.

"Fun, huh?" *Girl, you are dumber than dirt.* "Wow! Well, that's a wrap for me." I say while standing. I am too mentally drained to try and convince her that her husband is gay. She will come out of denial sooner or later, but it won't be on my watch. I grab a small business card off of my desk before walking Kimber to the door. We hug and then I hand her the card.

"What is this?" She asks.

"This is the number to the therapist I was telling you about a few weeks ago. Her name is Zenola Dawson and she has great credentials."

Looking completely stunned. "Willow, uhhh…what is this about? You are my therapist."

"No, Kimber, I'm not your therapist. I'm a life coach, and there are just some things that are outside of my realm. I think you're a wonderful person, but the issues you have are beyond my scope. You really need to talk to someone who has experience with family matters. Plus, I told you that I wanted to scale my business back and possibly start writing. I can't do that with the load that I'm carrying right now. Don't worry, you'll love Zenola. She's fabulous!" I reach out and pat her on the arm. Kimber steps towards me and gives me a big, hearty hug. "Gurrrl, I ain't gonna lie. I'm gonna miss you."

"I'll miss you, too, Kimber. Remember…"

"I know. I know. Always honor me!" She smiles and her face warms for a second.

"Put it to practice." I say, while giving her a serious glance.

"I will. I promise!" She says, while getting into her Benz. As she pulls off, I truly feel sorry for her. She's like millions of women that choose to overlook huge red flags, just to have a man in their lives. This is truly tragic.

I close the front door and slip out of my pumps before heading up the stairs. Before I reach the top of the staircase the phone rings. I do a quick jog to my bedroom and grab the phone before it goes to voicemail.

"*The Right Path*, how may I help you?"

"Hi, beautiful."

"Hi, babe. How are you?" I immediately start to blush.

"I'm good…really good. Why do you sound so breathy?"

"Oh, I had to run and catch the phone before it went to my answering service. Sorry," I reply.

"No problem. I like hearing you breathe heavy." Rece laughs.

"You sooooo nasty!" I chuckle. "We still on for tonight?"

"Yeah, why wouldn't we be?" He asks with concern.

"Well, you been so busy with work for the past few weeks that we haven't had much time together."

"I know, but I'm all caught up now. I'm all yours."

"That's good. What time should I be ready, love?"

"Seven o'clock, sharp. I have a limo picking you up, okay?"

"A limo, huh?" Silence. "Must be something special." Trying to get him to give some sort of hint, but it doesn't work.

"You'll have to show up and see for yourself."

We both laugh.

"Alright, love. I guess I'll see you in a few."

"I can't wait!" Rece replies.

"Love ya, babe!" I quickly interject before hanging up.

"Love you, more."

CHAPTER 36

I've been standing in my closet for nearly thirty minutes trying to decide what to wear on my date with Rece. I scan my color-coded attire one more time before deciding on this sexy number I was saving for a special occasion. It's a backless, knee length dress that plunges in the front, with extreme ruching that hugs every detail of my body. The dress is the color of Merlot wine. Journey would absolutely love this dress just for the color alone, considering it's her favorite.

I step into the dress and take a good, long look at my reflection. As I walk into my bathroom, I start pulling out the large, hot rollers from the top of my head and place them on my counter. Instead of combing my hair, I think I'll simply run my fingers through and allow the thick curls to land softly on my shoulders.

I'm not sure what Rece has in store for me, tonight, but I want to look incredibly hot. So, I think I'm gonna go light on the makeup and opt for some smoky eyes and a bold lip color. I grab my MAC bag and begin to apply my foundation. I've always loved getting dressed up and creating new looks. As a teen, I couldn't wait to get my first lipstick and eye shadow, but my mom was very strict about the fact that I had to be sixteen before I could wear any make-up. So, when my sixteenth birthday arrived, my mom presented me with a small, beautifully decorated box. I quickly yanked the bow and paper off and inside were the best gifts in the world, at least that's what I thought. It was only some Maybelline mascara and lip gloss that had a little bit of sparkle, but I thought I was the luckiest girl in town. Thus, began my obsession. I must admit, I have a huge fetish for lipstick. I probably own every color in the universe. I laugh at the thought. Just as I am applying my last bit of shadow, the phone rings. It's the driver of the limousine informing me that he is waiting outside. I tell him that I'll be out in just a few minutes.

I dash into my closet, again, grab my handbag and slip on a pair of hot, Casadel pumps. I look in the mirror one last time and smile. *Yeah, I think this look might leave him breathless…at least for a moment.* I chuckle.

I walk quickly down my stairs, being careful not to slip in these stilettos. That wouldn't be a pretty sight. I step outside and parked in front of my home is a stunning, platinum-colored Mercedes limo with a smooth, black top. It's striking, yet tasteful. It has Rece written all over it.

The driver is holding the door open for me. He's an older, white gentleman with noticeable gray hair peaking from the sides of his cap. He's handsome and looks as if he has taken good care of himself. He appears to be quite fit for his age. As I walk towards the limo, he welcomes me with a warm smile.

"Hello, Miss James. I'm George, and I'll be at your service this evening."

I return the smile. "Hi George." He extends his hand and helps me into the vehicle. "Thank you." I say.

"You're more than welcome, ma'am." George tips his hat slightly and closes my door. He gets into the limo and opens the small glass window. "Miss James, please help yourself to a beverage. There is wine to your left and bottled water to your right."

"Oh, thank you, George, but I'm fine."

"Okay, but let me know if you need anything."

"Well, you could start by telling me where we are going." I say before laughing.

"Ahhhhh, no ma'am. I've been sworn to secrecy. As a matter-of- fact, there's a scarf on the seat that you need to cover your eyes with before we get to our destination. Strict orders from Mr. Gallantine." George chuckles.

"Strict orders, huh?" I inquire.

"Yep." George quickly replies.

I grab the satin scarf and begin to place it over my eyes, but not before saying, "Okay, George, I'm gonna go along with all of this, but there had better not be any tricky stuff going on." I say, while smiling.

George lets out a hearty laugh. "No ma'am, you're in good hands. I promise."

I cover my eyes and lean back onto the soft leather. I feel myself getting butterflies. What in the world is Rece up to? He always has the best surprises. I clasp my hands together and place them on my lap before taking a deep breath. *Relax Willow…relax.*

Just then the car phone rings.

"Yes, sir…she's fine." Pausing. "Yes, she just put it on." Pausing, again. "We should be there in about fifteen minutes. Yes…yes. See you in a few. Bye." We begin driving to our secret destination. After about twenty minutes, I start tapping my foot out of nervousness.

"You okay, Miss James?" George asks with a concerned tone.

"Yes, sir, I'm fine. Just a little anxious, that's all." I reply.

"Well, don't be, we're almost there." I decide to sit quietly and just enjoy the ride. The music of Diana Krall is playing softly. I quietly sing to myself, "*Peel me a grape, crush me some ice, skin me a peach, save the fuzz for my pillow.*" The sunroof is open and I can smell the fresh night air. I like the feel of the soft wind gently blowing through my hair. My jazzy mood is interrupted when George says, "Here we are." His voice has a hint of excitement. I start to reach for my scarf and George immediately stops me.

"No, no, Miss James. Not yet. Behave yourself before you get us both in trouble." We both laugh. "Alright, I'll chill."

"Thank you, ma'am."

I feel the car come to a complete stop and I hear George getting out the vehicle. A few seconds later the door opens. The cool breeze brushes up against my leg.

"Your hand, Miss." I extend my hand and George guides me out of the limo. "Have a good evening, Miss James, Remember, do not remove the scarf until you're told." I hear George walking away from me.

"What? Are you leaving me, George?" Nothing… absolute silence. I hear the limo pull off. *Where am I? Shiiit, I'm taking this scarf off!* Before the thought fully takes flight, I hear some footsteps walking towards me, and then I feel him near me. He doesn't say a word. I know that he is taking in every ounce of me in with his eyes. I blush at the thought. He reaches out and caresses my shoulder and then proceeds to kiss my neck. Then he works his way up and gently nibbles on my ear lobe, before saying, "Damn it!" The heat of his breath sends a chill through me. I'm instantly overwhelmed by his nearness.

"Hiiiiiiii." I drag out, in a slow, molasses manner.

"Hello, gorgeous. How are you?"

"Ummm, I'm good…just curious."

"I bet you are. I know you were thinking about taking this scarf off." Rece chuckles and leans in closer. I become intoxicated by his scent. He's wearing one of my favorite colognes, Clive Christian 1872. Rece laughs and then removes the scarf from my eyes. It takes a minute for my eyes to adjust to the dusk.

We are standing in front of the Gallantine's private jet. It's a Gulfstream G650. We've taken a few trips in this luxury jet, and it is by far the ultimate standard when it comes to traveling. The aircraft can comfortably seat eighteen passengers, and can quickly be transformed to accommodate a business meeting, or a family dinner. Rece's family had the jet customized in cognac-colored Coach leather seating. The family logo is displayed throughout the plane on the bar, the glasses, and even the toilet paper. It is a beautiful piece of traveling luxury. Even though I've flown in it a couple of times; it always feels incredibly new and exciting. Rece, grabs my hands and leads me up the stairs into the jet.

CHAPTER 37

Now, this is very romantic. It takes my eyes a few seconds to adjust to the candlelit environment. Small, intimate containers, that give the illusion of candles, are flashing throughout the plane, and the beautiful, seductive music of Kem is playing. Rece walks me to my seat and proceeds to sit next to me. The Coach leather is divine, and I feel my body instantly relax at the feel and softness against my skin. I look over at Rece and smile.

Edwin Holt walks out from the cockpit and greets us, and asks Rece if we are ready to depart. "Absolutely." Rece says, before grabbing my hand and kissing it. Mr. Holt returns to the front of the plane and closes the doors behind him. He's been the Gallantine pilot for over ten years. Rece thinks quite highly of him.

"Miss Willow, are you enjoying yourself thus far?" Rece asks.

"Yes, I am. I must say that I was a little anxious after being blindfolded, but I knew I was in good hands, and that you wouldn't let any harm come my way."

"You are right, I will always protect you." He takes a deep breath. "You do believe that, don't you?"

"Of course I do, babe." I reply, as I look into his eyes and detect a level of seriousness.

"I'm glad." He says, before closing his eyes and allowing his head to fall back onto the seat.

Mr. Holt announces that we are about to depart and reminds us to fasten our seat belts before takeoff. We both check our seat belts to make sure they are secure.

I feel the plane start to move before it picks up to full speed. I chuckle as the plane lifts off the ground and causes butterflies to erupt in my stomach. Rece reaches over and grabs my hand until we've reached a comfortable cruising altitude of thirty-thousand feet. The pilot shuts off the "fasten seat belt" sign and tells us to make ourselves comfortable and enjoy the flight.

Rece unbuckles his seat belt, gets up and sits in the seat directly in front of me. He leans back and clasps his hands between his legs, while giving me this devilish grin.

"Mr. Gallantine, what are you up to?" I ask. "Because, I know you're up to something." I continue with an air of certainty.

"Who, me?" While pointing to himself.

"Yes, darling, you." I reply, before we both start laughing. Rece then leans forward and unbuckles my seatbelt, before getting on his knees and grabbing me around my waist. He pulls me tightly towards him and plants a gentle kiss on my forehead.

"God, I love you, woman." He whispers.

"I love you, too, baby." I respond with care. Then I kiss his lovely lips. I feel Rece squeeze me tighter, as if for dear life. So, I place my hands on his face, look deep into his eyes and ask, "Rece, honey, what's wrong?

"He looks at me and smiles before responding, "Absolutely nothing. Everything…I mean everything, is perfect!"

I continue to look at him with concern. "Okay, but…" He places a finger on my lips.

"Shhh…, I have something I want to say to you."

"Okay." I say, before sitting up straight and at full attention.

While still on his knees, Rece reaches into his pocket and pulls out a small, black velvet box and opens it. I gasp. Inside of the box is the most beautiful ring I have ever seen. *I can't believe this! Is this really happening?*

"Oh my god, Rece!" I scream. "I can't…"

"No, baby, please don't say anything, just listen… please." He says, as a tear rolls down his cheek. I reach to wipe it away, while trying to contain this wave of emotion that I am feeling. I can feel my heart starting to race. I have so much to say, but I sit in silence as Rece begins to pour out his heart out to me.

"Willow, I don't even know where to begin. First, let me start by saying that I am completely in love with you. You have captured my attention from day one, and each moment that I have spent in your presence has been a blessing and privilege." He pauses for a moment. "All of my life I have been searching for someone to love me for me. Not for my name or status, but just for me. Someone that could love me in spite of my faults. Someone that could enjoy my company in silence. Someone that could smile at me and make me forget all of my worries. Someone that could turn me on with a simple touch. You are that someone." He pauses again

175

to take a deep breath. "Will you make my heart whole? Will you marry me?"

Through both of our tears of joy I manage to say, "Ohhh baby, of course I'll marry you. Oh my, this is unbelievable!" We stand and embrace before engaging in the most romantic kiss ever. There are no words that can express this very moment. It's beyond happiness.

We run into a bit of turbulence that shakes us apart. The pilot announces that it was just a small pocket of turbulence and that the rest of our trip should be smooth. We laugh and take our seats, again. Our smiles could light up the entire world. Rece takes the ring out of the box and places it on my finger.

"Rece, this is absolutely beautiful. It's perfect!" I take a long look at this stunning diamond before looking up at Rece.

"Do you like it?" He asks.

"I love it! But more than anything, I love you. Rece, you are my joy. My life has been filled with so much happiness since we started dating, and I can't imagine spending the rest of my life with anyone other than you. You are my dream come true."

"Likewise." He replies, before lifting me from my seat to engage in another passionate kiss.

"Whew, you better stop this. I know you're not trying to start anything on this jet?" We both laugh.

"Alright, I'll chill for now, but you are looking really hot in this dress. I can't help myself." He says, before tapping me on the ass. I sit down and take another look at my ring. *Damn, this man has good taste!*

"I can't wait to tell my parents!" I exclaim.

Rece smiles at me before saying, "Mmmm, they already know."

"What? How?" I ask in shock.

"I had lunch with your parents and asked them for your hand in marriage." He says.

"What did they say?" I ask with anticipation.

"Well, your dad said, "Hell no!" Rece says with a tone of seriousness.

"Really?" I ask. "Are you serious?"

Rece tries to keep a serious face but realizes that he can't, and bursts into laughter. "Nah, babe. I'm just kidding. They gave us their blessings."

"Whew! You had me worried there for a sec." I motion as if I am wiping my brow.

"No worries, me and Pops are alright." He chuckles.

"Pops, huh?" I laugh at the thought. *My dad will have a white son-in-law...how funny.*

"Yeah, that's my guy. He's good people and he has a hell of a fine daughter!" We both crack up.

"Rece, thanks for making me the happiest woman in the world."

"My pleasure, future Mrs. Gallantine."

My heart and soul warm at the thought.

CHAPTER 38

Wow! She said yes. Damn it, this feels so good! Rece and Willow Gallantine. Yeah, it has a nice ring to it. I let several minutes go by to allow Willow and I the opportunity to bask in our newfound glow. Neither of us can stop smiling. I tell Willow that I need to go to the bathroom and excuse myself. I slide the partition screen apart and head to the back of the plane. Waiting patiently are two exquisite gifts for Willow. I want this evening to be a night that she will never forget.

"Hello, ladies," I say in a low, kind tone, "I hope I haven't kept you waiting too long?" The two of them look striking in their white, Egyptian robes. The contrast of the white against their lovely tones is very sexy.

"Hi, Mr. Gallantine." They both say in breathy unison.

The sepia brown jewel pulls her robe apart to reveal a set of oiled, toned legs that would give Tina Turner a run for her money. *Nice.* She giggles and says, "Not at all." Revealing a slight Jamaican accent. She then leans back and allows me a slight peak at her heaven. "I'm Bella."

Not to be outdone, the copper-colored delight allows her robe to gracefully fall from her shoulders, revealing perfectly sculpted 38D breasts. *Delightful.* "It's our pleasure. I'm Eva."

She says, with a hint of Spanish accent before giving me a wink.

"Mmmm, okay, ladies," shaking my head. "Give me a few minutes and I'll be back to get you."

"We'll be waiting." Miss Legs replies. I grab both of their hands and place a soft peck on each. "See you in a few. Damn!"

I head back to the front of the plane to check on Willow. She is glowing.

"Hey, you," I say, before kissing the top of her head.

"Hey," she says, before looking up at me. "You okay?" She asks with care.

"Yeah, babe, I'm cool. I'm perfect." Smiling.

"Well, alright handsome. How about we toast?"

"I thought you'd never ask. I brought a little something special for this special occasion." I reach over and grab the two champagne glasses from the bar and hand one to Willow, before revealing the bottle that's been chilling on ice.

Willow breaks into a huge grin, "Ohhh, honey, Armand De Brignac. You know I love this rose'. Man, you are good."

"Yeah, I wanted this night to be unforgettable." Pausing slightly. "How am I doing so far?" I ask, before filling our glasses.

"So far, so good!" Willow lifts her glass. "To the man of my dreams, and our wonderful future together. I love you!"

"I love you, too." I reply. "Oh, I almost forgot, I have one more surprise for you." I say sheepishly.

Taking another sip from her glass. "Really? I don't know if I can handle anything else."

"Ohhh, I think you can handle what I have in store for you," I say before chuckling.

Willow leans in closer to me and says, "Mmmm, sounds kinky." She laughs.

"You have no idea," I respond.

"Well, you know me. Bring it on, Big Daddy!"

"Okay, Little Mama, but first, let me taste those lips, again." We lean closer and connect. Our tongues come together and dance a slow, melodic tango. The lingering taste of the rose' adds a delicate sweetness. *Exhilirating.*

CHAPTER 39

I'm not sure if there are any words that can fully describe my sense of joy right now. I am beyond happy. This night is turning out to be way more than I ever imagined. It is truly one of the best moments in my life. I mean, really? How often does someone get blindfolded, whisked away and proposed to on a private jet? Not often, I'm sure!

I am so in love with Rece. This is really an awesome relationship, and tonight he has really blown me away. I really don't think that anything else can top tonight, except the wedding itself and the birth of our first child. He'd love to hear me say that. He can't wait to be a father. I knew that our relationship had become serious, and we had even discussed marriage on a few occasions. However, I really thought it would be another year before Rece popped the question. I figured that he would wait a while like most men. I don't know why I thought that, considering he has never done anything remotely close to the other guys I've dated. Maybe that explains all of our recent dialogue on family and the specific roles of husbands and wives. Rece and I are both very traditional when it comes to family structure, and we see eye-to-eye on most things.

There was however, one area where our experiences were completely different, and that was church. I grew up in church. I don't know anything else. I can't remember a time in my life when the church wasn't an intricate part of my family. Rece, on the other hand, attended church sporadically, and it wasn't something that was mandatory. He has gone to church more since he started dated me than he has in his entire life. So, it was something that I knew we would get around to discussing. He did suggest that we look at attending a more diverse place of worship once we got married, and I agreed.

I would feel strange being the only black face in a congregation too. So, I can totally understand Rece wanting to see a few of his people when he goes to worship. Plus, when we have children it will be important for them to feel welcomed. Not that an all-black church wouldn't welcome biracial children, but it would be nice for our children to interact with kids that look like them, or with kids that are a product of two races.

Oh well, I guess we'll cross that hurdle when we get to it. For now, I am just going to enjoy this incredible evening. In my heart I have always known that Rece was the one, but I didn't want to get ahead of myself. I made a conscious decision to stay in the moment, and allow each day to unfold. I really wanted us to grow as friends, and not just allow our sexual energy to consume the relationship. Although I must say, my baby has some good nookie.

It's been a wonderful ride, and I am soooo looking forward to being Mrs. Rece Gallantine. Whew! Thank you, Lord! Thank you for healing my heart and allowing me to love, again. *What's taking Rece so long?* As I turn toward the back of the plane, I see Rece walking back to me. I stand and reach for him.

"Hey, babe, what took you so long?"

He smiles a devilish grin and says, "I told you that I had another surprise for you."

"Ohhh, you do, huh?" I ask, while grabbing his ass. He pulls me closer to him and I feel his cock start to rise.

"Yes, I do, but first I need for you to lie back, close your eyes and relax. Okay?" Rece fully reclines my seat, and allows his hands to gently brush across my breast. My body experiences an instant shiver.

"Okay!" I say with a hint of excitement, before relaxing my entire body into the plush leather.

"Are you ready, baby?" His voice is low and sexy.

I start to respond, but he immediately kisses me and my mind goes into a zone.

"Mmmm, I like." I purr.

"Yeah, me, too." He whispers. "Now, don't open your eyes until I say so."

"Okay."

"Promise?"

"I promise." I say, in a barely audible tone. Then I close my eyes.

"THE MAIN COURSE"

CHAPTER 40

Rece grabs my head and begins to gently run his fingers through my loose curls. His hands slide down my neck and shoulders, before sliding my dress off. I lift my hips slightly to simplify his task, and reveal my hairless kitty. Rece spreads my legs open and lets out a sigh, "Ahhh, just the way I like it." He says, before softly stroking the top of my mound. I giggle at the gentle tickle, and gasp when I feel his tongue caress my clit's protective shell.

"Mmmm, yeah, baby." I sigh.

"You like this?"

"I do, I really do." Panting.

"Good, I want you to enjoy every minute of this evening." Rece whispers.

"So far, so good." I reply with closed eyes. And that's when it happened. I feel Rece's hands pull away from me, and then I feel an incredibly soft pair of hands start to caress my thighs, followed by another set of equally soft hands that start massaging my breasts. *Is this what I think it is? Oh my god, this is some wild shit!* I take a deep breath to adjust to this newfound sensation. God, I want to open my eyes so badly, but I promised Rece I would oblige his request. The delicate hands on my thighs move up and begin to stroke my ass.

Then someone licks my lips and begins to softly nibble my bottom lip, before spreading them apart with their tongue. The kiss is gentle, soft…sweet. It's different from kissing Rece. It's yummy in a different kind of way. I sigh, again.

"Open your eyes, babe." Rece says.

I slowly open my eyes and am delighted to see such beautiful women in front of me. *Shiiit, if I'm gonna be done by some women they need to be fine as fuck, and I must say that these women are hot!* I instantly begin to blush.

"Hi, Willow I'm Bella." The chocolate darling says, revealing a perfect smile, while continuing to caress my breasts.

I turn toward the copper jewel. She introduces herself and then begins kissing me.

"Uhhhh, mmmm…" I can't seem to find the right words to say. Eva places a finger over my lips, "Relax, beautiful one. We're here to delight you, okay?" I simply nod and look over at Rece. He smiles, "You okay?"

I wink. "Yeah, baby, I'm good." I say. I am sure by now, I have turned completely red.

"Enough said," Rece replies, "Let the fun begin."

Eva doesn't waste any time. She grabs my ass and pulls me closer to her. First, she rubs her hands between my legs, ever so gently allowing her fingers to brush over my heavenly paradise. I feel my pussy respond to her feminine touch. She inserts her middle finger, and tactfully teases my G-spot. When she sees my body trimble with delight, she pulls her finger out and slowly licks my precious juices off her finger. "Ohhh, my beauty, this pussy is ripe." Eva spreads my sugar walls and begins to lick my treasure in a slow, melodic manner…never missing a beat. Her licks are long and precise. She circles my clit with tender care, as not to surprise my tiny friend before its time. Then, I feel her tongue begin to dart in and out of my pussy, creating the most wonderful sensation.

"Mmmm, that feels good." I say, before Eva decides to take my pussy to a whole new level. She starts to suck my clit. Her lips are soft and her tongue, even softer. I let out a sigh, and lift my hips to meet her amazing mouth. She then proceeds to do a vacuum-sucking motion on my clit. It is so intense! I grab Bella's leg. She smiles at me before taking both of my erect nipples into her mouth.

Rece gets up from his seat and walks towards me. He doesn't say a word, he simply kisses me. I literally want to scream, but my mind, my body, my words---are all in a powerful place of passion. I fiercely grab Eva's head, and begin pumping my pussy to meet each one of her intense sucks. I feel my body about to explode as never before.

Rece instructs Bella to play with my ass. She quickly joins her partner. As Eva occupies my clit, Bella inserts her finger into my soaking wet hideaway and begins teasing my G-spot. "Uhhh, ohhh my God!" I scream. Bella continues to play until I'm literally climbing the walls. Once her fingers are drenched with my sweet juices, she inserts a finger slowly into my ass. I literally go into a fog of ecstasy.

I am fucking Eva's face, and with each thrust Bella allows her finger to thrust deeper into my ass. *I am fucking gone!* My body is paralyzed with pleasure. I feel my pussy pulsing with delight before my walls explode with a volcanic rush of wetness.

"Ohhh fuck, Rece, ohhh!'

"Yeah, baby, get this shit!" Rece chimes.

"Oh yeah, you've got some nice pussy on you." Bella purrs, before pushing Eva to the side, straddling me and allowing our clits to meet. *This shit cannot be happening!*

Fucking Rece is absolute heaven, but this shit is indescribable. It's so fucking erotic. We continue to slowly grind our pussies together, before Rece decides that he's had enough. He pulls his dick out, Eva grabs it and begins giving him a blow job that nearly tops my shit. I mean, I am impressed with her dick sucking skills, but when it comes to sucking Rece Gallantine's dick; I am the fucking BOSS!

Bella sits up, we embrace and begin to engage in a very intimate kiss. I begin caressing her body. She's soft, yet tight. She pulls me closer and our breasts meet. It produces a butterfly sensation when our nipples collide, and we giggle with delight. I reach between her legs and feel her wetness. It's the first time that I have ever felt a vagina other than mine. It's warm, wet and soft. *Now, I understand why men want their dicks in such a special place. I guess if I had a dick, I'd want it in a wet, pussy too!*

Bella spreads her legs to allow my finger complete entry. "More," she says. I insert another finger and she whispers once again, "More." I insert a third finger, and she says, "Ahhh, that's it." She moans, as she tightens her walls around my fingers. Bella then removes my hand, places it up to her mouth, and begins to devour each finger with delicate licks. When she is finished, she grabs my face and kisses me. "Nice, huh?" She asks. I nod and smile.

Just when I think it can't get any better, Rece gives Eva a time-out from of his dick and grabs me from Bella. He bends me over, and begins fucking me from behind. Not wanting to be left out, the two hotties start pleasuring each other in a beautiful sixty-nine. The sight of such naughtiness, and being thoroughly fucked, is too much. All of my senses are in an ultimate heavenly state.

The plane hits another bit of turbulence, but Rece doesn't let go of my ass. Instead he goes deeper with each bump, sending my pussy into an unknown zone. I can't help but go to church.

"Oh, God! Oh, God! Help me, Lord…"

CHAPTER 41

"Girl, get the fuck outta here! He what? You are lying, Willow!"

"I am soooo serious, Journey. It was the most sensational night of my life. I mean, I was already blown away when Rece proposed, but when I opened my eyes and saw those two women; I knew I was in for the night of my life."

"Oooh, girl, I am so jealous. Rece is the fucking man!" Journey responds with sheer excitement.

"I know, huh?" I reply.

"So, when am I going to see this fabulous ring? When is the date? What colors are you going with?" Journey asks, without pausing for air.

I laugh. "Hold on, little mama. I just got engaged last night, and we haven't had a chance to talk about any of that stuff."

"Well, I already know that I'm the maid of honor. Please pick out a fly dress for me, okay? Don't be trying to cover me up. I need some of this sexiness to show when I walk down the aisle." We both burst into laughter.

"You are a mess, Journey. I promise that your dress will be fly."

"Thank you. Because I've been in few weddings where the dresses were a hot mess."

"You know I wouldn't do that to you, pooh."

"I know, girl, I'm just trippin'. On a serious note, I am so happy for you. I mean if anyone deserves this, you do. You are such a loving and kind individual, and I know you're going to make Rece a wonderful wife. I can't wait for the wedding, and for you to have some babies that I can spoil."

"Chile, can I get to the altar first?"

"Oh yeah, I forgot about that." We both laugh. "Plus, I can't wait to see Jordan's face when he finds out. He is going to trip."

"He shouldn't trip. I gave Jordan many opportunities to get it right, and he didn't. Shit, you snooze you lose!"

"I know that's right, Willow." She chuckles. "Now, I know that your parents know about the engagement, but what about Rece's parents?"

Pausing slightly. "Well, he told his brother and sister-in-law, he plans to tell his parents on Thanksgiving Day. They always have a big family gathering and he wants me and my parents to come."

"How do you think his family is going to respond? Especially his mom, since he bypassed all of her picks."

"I'm not sure, I just hope it goes better than when Rece met my dad." Laughing. "Whew, I'll never forget that night. I am so glad that Dad ended up liking Rece, because it would be very, very difficult to marry someone that my dad didn't care for."

"Well, I think his parents will love you, and his mom will love having you as a daughter-in-law."

"I hope so, I really hope so." I reply, with a tinge of uncertainty.

In her normal energetic tone, she replies, "They will! Well, I know you have a lot of things to do today. How about we hook up at Starbucks in Green Hills for an evening latte, around six?"

"That'll work, doll."

"Okay, I'll see you then. Bye."

"Later, chick." I reply.

I hang up the phone and dash to the bathroom to put on my running gear. I think I'll knock out five miles today. I pause for a moment and take a deep breath. I can still smell Rece. I notice his dress shirt is strewn across the tub. I reach for it and place the gently-starched shirt against my face. *Mmmm, that's my baby*. The phone rings again.

"Hello."

"Hi, beautiful." It's Rece.

"Hi, honey. Where are you?"

"I just finished working out and am about to get something to eat."

"Oh, okay. That's why you woke up so early."

"Yeah, I needed to get one in today. I was so busy this week running around to get everything in order for last night, that I didn't get a chance to go to the gym."

"Well, the time away was worth it." I say.

"I know, I would do it again if I had to."

"I'm sure you would, tiger." We laugh in unison.

"So, what's your day like?" Rece asks,

"I'm about to go for a run, and then I have a few errands to take care of before I meet Journey for coffee this evening."

"Okay, call me later. Tell Journey hello for me."

"I will." I reply.

"I love you."

"I love you, too, Rece."

CHAPTER 42

Since Willow is out doing her thing, I think I'll swing by my parents' home and check on them. I got a chance to see my dad briefly at the beginning of the week. He was complaining that my mom was already planning Thanksgiving dinner, even though it is three weeks away. He said that it just didn't take this much preparation for some turkey, dressing, sweet potatoes and green bean casserole. I laughed, because he complains about Mom and her planning every holiday season. Why doesn't he just go with the flow? The holidays are her "thing" and she always goes all out.

I actually get a kick out of seeing her so excited and at the end of the day. She really does know how to entertain, and she's a pretty good cook. I can't wait to eat some of her sweet potatoes. I think I will ask her to share her recipe with Willow once we're married. Mom claims that she'll go to her grave with the family recipe. She's a trip, but I love her dearly.

I use my key to let myself in. Mom has some Frank Sinatra playing, and I can hear her trying to belt out the classic standard, "I love Paris in the springtime, I love Paris in the fall, I love…" Pausing mid-line as she sees me in the foyer. "Oh, hi, sweetheart. Come on in here and help your mama open these boxes."

As I walk into the dining room, I notice she has boxes everywhere. "I ordered some new holiday decorations." She says, while unwrapping two beautiful bronze urns. "Ohhh, Rece, aren't these fabulous? I had these custom-made for the porch area. They are going to look stunning with all of the beautiful mums and Mexican sage that Sergio will be planting next week. I absolutely love them! And this patina bronze is perfect for the fall." She is smiling, as if someone has given her a billion dollars. The urns are quite nice, but I'm not sure it requires all of this. "Yes, Mom, they are lovely." I lean in and kiss her on the cheek. "How are you, beautiful?"

Beaming. "Wonderful…simply wonderful!"

"I can see that." I reply, before taking a seat next to the stacked boxes.

My mom places each urn on the floor near the French doors, before turning towards me and handing me a box cutter.

"Here." She motions to the boxes in front of me. "Open that box on the top." She points. "I hope that's the box with my tablecloth and napkins." I proceed to follow her directive and sure enough, it's her linens. I pull one of the napkins out of its protective guard. "Ahhh, Mom, these are really nice. I like the colors. Nice." The silk blend linens echo the colors of fall in a lavish tapestry.

"They are perfect! I think everything is coming together nicely. Yes, indeed." She says, while grabbing the napkin from my hand and quickly examining it. I decide to continue opening boxes before being told. Her excitement grows with each revealed piece.

"Where is Dad?" I ask.

"He and your Uncle Lou took the boat out this morning. I told them it was too cold to be fishing, but they wanted to get one last catch in before the weather really turns." She replied.

"That sounds nice. I haven't gone fishing in a while. That's something I really enjoy."

"Yeah, you and Bronson loved being out on the water. Plus, you guys used to catch the biggest fish." She chuckles at the memory.

"I know, we were pretty good." I smile.

Reaching over and patting me on the head. "You guys should start doing it, again."

"You're right. Hopefully, when things slow down, we'll be able to enjoy some of our pastimes. Bronson has been busy at the office. Plus, he and Mindy are trying to finalize their adoption." The mention of the adoption brings an instant warmth to my mom's face.

"Oh, I know. I can't wait to see my new grandbaby. At least my younger son loves me." She laughs, and then winks at me.

I start laughing because I know where she is trying to go with this little jab. "In due time Mom…in due time." I take a deep breath. "As a matter of fact, I'm working on that." She stops and places her new serving dish on the dining table.

"What did you say? Did I hear you correctly?" She asks, with a pensive look.

"Yes, Mom." I reply, with a sly grin.

She pulls out a chair and plops down. "You're dating someone?"

"Yes, Mom, I am."

"For how long? Who is she? Who are her people?" It's obvious that she is completely stunned at the news.

I pat her hand. "Whoa, slow down, Mom. You'll meet her soon. I plan on inviting Willow and her parents to Thanksgiving dinner." I wait for her dramatic response.

"What?" She throws her hands up.

"Is that okay with you?" I ask.

She hits the table. "Goddamn it, Rece! You know I don't like surprises. I like for things to be planned. Who is this Willow? What kind of name is Willow? Who names their child after a tree? Is she pretty? God, let her be pretty because I don't want any ugly grandbabies." I wait for her to finally stop with the barrage of questions. I get up and walk to the other side of the table and sit next to her.

"Mom, she's beautiful, and her parents are lovely people. You're going to love Willow once you get to know her, I promise." I grab her hands. I can tell that she isn't totally convinced.

"Have you told your dad yet?"

"Not yet, that's why I stopped by today. I wanted to tell the both of you."

"Well, I can't wait until he hears that our eldest son is dating." She starts clapping her hands. "There is a God! Come here."

I lean forward and she kisses me on the cheek. "You have made your mom a very happy woman. I had almost given up on you. Shit, I was starting to think you were gay

199

since you passed up all of the wonderful suitors I introduced you to."

I give her a stern look. "Really, Mom?"

"Yes, really." She bursts into laughter.

"Well, I'm not gay."

"Thank goodness. That would kill your dad." I laugh, but in all seriousness, it would kill my dad if any of his sons were gay. He is "Mr. Homophobic". "I just hadn't met the right one, until now." I blush at the thought of my new fiance'.

"The right one?" She probes.

"Yeah, she is." I break into a huge smile. I can't contain it.

"Well, hot damn! Rece Gallantine is in love!"

"Very much so." I concur.

Mom stands up. "I need a glass of wine. This is too much this early in the morning. How long did you say you've been dating?"

"I didn't." I reply.

"How long, son?" She asks, with a hint of sternness, while picking up the tablecloth.

"Almost a year." I brace myself.

"What? And you're just mentioning this to me?" She throws the tablecloth down.

I give her a serious look. "Mom, calm down. I wanted to be sure before I introduced Willow to the family. Okay?"

She gives me one of those I could slap you looks. "Okay, son, but this doesn't sit well with me."

I get up, walk towards her and put my arms around her. She tries to wiggle away from me, but I pull her in closer. "Just be happy for me, Victoria Gallantine." I kiss her on her forehead.

"Okay, my handsome boy." She says with some reluctance.

"Now let's finish opening up your stuff." I say, while grabbing the box cutter. I glance at my mom and she's smiling. That makes me very happy.

CHAPTER 43

Gosh, the weeks have flown by. I can't believe it's already Thanksgiving Day. I've been preparing for this moment for quite some time now. I am meeting Rece's parents for the first time. I can't say that I'm nervous, but maybe a little anxious. Meeting someone's parents is always a big deal. It can go extremely well or it could blow up in your face. Hopefully, this meeting will be pleasant.

I'm sort of glad that it's happening on Thanksgiving Day, because my parents are coming along, and it will really be a family affair.

I've been probing Rece about his parents and he assures me that they're down-to-earth folk, but his mom is a socialite. He says that once you get past her pomp and circumstance, she's a real sweetheart. I'm also really excited about meeting my future niece. Bronson and Mindy received their newborn a few days ago and plan on bringing her to the family gathering. It will be the first opportunity for the entire family to meet the new edition. I'm sure everyone wanted to run over to their house on the day the baby arrived, but the family agreed that the new parents needed time alone. I think that was best. Mya, that's my new future niece's name. I like it. I bet she's a cutie pie.

Rece squeezes my hand. "You alright? What are you thinking about?"

Snapping out of my daze. "Oh, sweetheart, I'm fine." I squeeze his hand back to assure him, and then turn to look at my parents in the backseat. They are engrossed in some video game on my mom's phone. My mom looks up and winks at me. I immediately feel myself calming down.

"Here we are everyone!" Rece says. As he drives down the winding road that leads to his parents' mansion. It's simply breathtaking. The 20,000 square foot Mediterranean home is exquisite. Now, I can see firsthand where Rece gets his talent. The attention to detail on the outside of this home can only boast something incredible on the inside. The driveway has several parked cars, so I assume that everyone must be here. Rece parks next to a sparkling, silver McLaren MP4-12C. *Wow! Someone has good taste. One of my former clients has one of these 593-hp supercars. It drives like heaven. Not many people know that I have a passion for cars. Especially fast ones!*

"You ready?" Rece asks.

"Yep, I'm ready." I reply.

Rece gets out, and opens the door for my parents, and then comes around to my side. He gently grabs my hand, to assist me in standing, before placing my arm under his. He leads us towards the sophisticated, grand entrance. It's beautifully decorated. Rece opens the front door and allows each of us to step into the foyer. Before I enter, my eyes land upon the ornate light fixture on both sides of the masculine door. They are identical to the fixtures at my parents' home.

Once we're inside, we can hear voices and jazz playing softly. Rece hangs our coats in the coat closet and leads us into the formal living room where everyone is gathered.

The Gallantine's home is meticulously designed for entertaining. The open floor plan allows for each room to be connected in a unique way that promotes warmth. The walls are adorned with art that they've collected over the years, including original pieces by Andy Warhol. There is one wall that is comprised of lovely photos of Rece and Bronson, from birth to adulthood. I can immediately sense that the Gallantines adore their boys. The high arches, decorative columns and custom hand-laid tiles just further accentuate the detail to excellence.

As we get closer to the living area...I count; four handsome, aged men and three equally attractive, older women. The ladies are all blond and botoxed, with heavy make-up, yet impeccably dressed.

Our entrance prompts a quick silence amongst the group. All eyes are on the African Americans with Rece.

"Happy Thanksgiving, everyone!" Rece enthusiastically greets the small crowd.

"Happy Thanksgiving." Everyone replies in unison. The cheerful tones that we heard when we first entered have certainly become sombered. We are clearly the center of attention.

"Family, I'd like to introduce you to my fiancé, Willow James and her parents Mr. and Mrs. James."

Someone coughs, and then the smiles quickly turn to shocked expressions. One of the men start walking towards us, and I immediately see the resemblance. It's Rece's dad. "Hi, son." He gives Rece a hearty hug.

"Hi, Dad." Rece replies.

"Well, hello pretty lady," he reaches for my hand and places a soft kiss on top, "It's a pleasure to meet my future daughter-in-law."

"It is a pleasure to meet you sir," I reply. He turns and pats Rece on the back. "Son, you did good!" He says, before taking a few steps towards my parents.

"Mr. and Mrs. James, welcome to our home!" He shakes my dad's hand, and then obliges my mom with a slightly longer kiss to her hand. She smiles, as not to appear overly flattered. "Our pleasure," Dad replies.

I'm sure my dad picked up on this, because nothing gets passed him. However, he'll let it slide to keep the peace for tonight. But, I can hear him when he gets home tonight, "Baby, did you see how long that mutha' fucka' took to kiss your hand?" I laugh to myself at the thought.

"Well, make yourself at home. These old geezers are Rece's uncles, Louis, Andy and Frank, and these three jewels are their wives, Friday, Debra and Zannavia."

Mr. Gallantine says, while walking back to the bar. The wives haven't moved since Rece made the announcement. Finally, one of the women breaks away from the group.

"Hello, darling! What a pleasant surprise." She smiles at me and extends her hand.

"Did I hear you correctly, nephew? Engaged?" Puzzled.

"Yes, Aunt Deb."

"Well, just how long have the two of you been dating?" She asks with a slight attitude.

"Almost a year, auntie." Rece smiles.

"A year! And we're just meeting her? Rece!"

Rece hugs his aunt and then kisses her on the cheek. "Just be happy for me okay?"

His aunt tries to ask more questions, but Rece cuts her short and tells her we're going to meet the rest of the family. Everyone is pleasant, not overly friendly, but not rude. We engage in the normal pleasantries. Are you from Nashville? Where did you go to school? What do you do?

As we engage in casual chitchat, a well-starched waiter approaches and offers each of us a glass of wine. We gladly accept, as Mr. Gallantine offers us a seat. Just as we're all about to sit down I hear a lively, southern voice, "My, my... what is all of the commotion about?" A beautiful or shall I say, stunning woman walks in the room. She removes her apron to reveal a small, toned figure. Her eyes immediately lock with mine. She sees her son's arm around my waist and she knows. She makes no adjustment to contain her shock and obvious disdain.

"Rece, who are these people?" She questions in a curt, molasses tone.

Rece pulls me closer. "Mom, this is Willow." Unable to contain his excitement.

"Uhhh...what?" She darts her eyes towards Mr. Gallantine. He chuckles at her sense of uneasiness. Her face begins to redden. Realizing that she's about to lose her cool, she quickly makes an adjustment. A woman of her pedigree would certainly not let anyone see her sweat. She takes a deep breath, exhales and extends her hand in my direction. I smile graciously as she takes in every ounce of me.

"Well," pausing slightly, "Hello, Miss Willow. It's very nice to finally meet you. Welcome to our Thanksgiving dinner." Her manicured hands are delicate, almost fragile to the touch. "Thank you, Mrs. Gallantine. It's a pleasure meeting you, as well."

"And these are Willow's lovely parents, Mr. and Mrs. James." Rece stretches his arm in the direction of my parents. Dad and Mom take a few steps towards Mrs. Gallantine.

"Mr. and Mrs. James, it's so nice to meet you both." They proceed to shake hands.

"Please, call us Walter and Wilhemina." My father replies, while still holding onto her hand. It appears the handshake from my dad startled her slightly.

"Uhhh, well...uhhh, since we're gonna be family, why not?" Mrs. Gallantine grabs the wine glass out of my dad's hand and chugs down the whole thing. My mom is clearly stunned, but she stays cool.

"There!" Mrs. Gallantine finishes off the last drop of wine and hands the glass back to my dad.

"Honey!" Looking over at Mr. Gallantine. "Fix Mr. James...I mean Walter another drink! Excuse me for a moment." She walks quickly out of the room and down the hallway. I look at Rece. "Babe, is everything okay, or should we go?"

"Sweetheart, everything is fine. I told you that my mom can be quite the drama queen. Give her a few minutes and she'll be fine."

I'm not totally convinced. "Are you sure, Rece?"

"I'm positive. Now, let's relax and enjoy the evening." We make ourselves comfortable on the beautiful paisley sofa, while the aunts whisk my mom off into the kitchen.

"Walter, come on over here and let me fix you a real drink. You look like you might enjoy a nice, aged cognac." Mr. Gallantine motions for my dad to join them at the bar.

Rece opens the center ottoman and pulls out a family photo album. We flip through each, aged plastic page, as he gives me the intimate details of his childhood. He and his brother appear to be incredibly happy and loved in the photos. I laugh when I see Rece in his official Boy Scouts uniform. He was a handsome boy.

He nudges me. "Don't laugh babe, you see I had a little swagger with badges and all."

"You had something, but I wouldn't call it swagger." We both laugh. Rece leans in and kisses me softly on the lips.

"I love you, Rece Gallantine."

"Me too."

CHAPTER 44

The evening is progressing smoothly. It took Mom a few minutes to gain her composure, but when she finally came back into the living room, she was a new woman. Bright. Bubbly. Gracious. The total hostess. I'm more than positive that she went into her room and popped a few Xanex pills. She's always happier after she's had one or two.

Mom plops down on the sofa next to Willow, and begins to tell her about one of the photos.

"Ohhh, Willow, this is Rece's fifth birthday party. Isn't he adorable?"

Willow nods. "He was just the sweetest little boy ever. I never had any problems out of my little darling, Rece. That is until he became a teenager and then he was hell on wheels!" Mom breaks into a hearty laugh, and then glances at her watch. "I wonder where Bronson is?" She says out loud, but not really aiming the question at anyone in particular.

"Sooo, darling, how exactly did you meet my son?" She asks in her most southern molasses tone, while gently touching the sleeve of Willow's dress. Her touch may appear friendly, but in actuality, she's examining the fabric to ensure its not a knock-off Michael Kors. My mom isn't slick, she's slowing trying to size Willow.

Willow clears her throat. "Well, Mrs. Gallantine, I actually met Rece at…" The doorbell rings. I get up from the sofa to open the door. It's Bronson and Mindy. They are both glowing. Their happiness cannot be contained. I'm excited! Bronson and I embrace, and I kiss Mindy on the cheek.

"It's about time, Bronson. We were all wondering if you guys were going to stand us up on Thanksgiving."

"Nah, we just had to get the baby situated."

"Speaking of the baby, can her Uncle Rece finally see her?" I ask, while reaching for the covered carrier.

Bronson blocks my arm. "Hold on, Uncle Rece, let us hang our coats and we'll be right in."

"Alright, but hurry up." I walk back into the living room and let everyone know that Bronson and his family will be in shortly. Everyone is ecstatic. Bronson and Mindy enter the room within seconds of my announcement. Bronson places the baby carrier on the loveseat. "Oh, hurry up, Bronson, let me see my grandbaby for Christ's sake!" Mom says, with pride and excitement.

"Everyone, I'd like for you to meet the newest member of the family, Mya Victoria Gallantine!" Bronson removes the blanket from the carrier and lifts out the most beautiful baby in the world. She has a head full of black, curly locks and the brightest brown eyes I've ever seen. She squirms and then gives us all a slight smile as if she's saying, "Hi, everyone, I'm finally here!"

"Ohhh, she is so pretty, Mindy." Willow says.

"Ahhh, she's black! My granddaughter is black? Oh, God!" My mom screams, before fainting and falling to the floor. My aunts all rush over to assist.

"Vikki, darling are you okay?" Aunt Zannavia asks with concern.

"Vic, wake up, sweetheart." Chimes Aunt Deb.

The men don't budge. They are used to Mom and all of her drama. Aunt Friday is frozen in place, her eyes are fixed on baby Mya. My uncles start re-filling their glasses, and Mr. and Mrs. James both have WTF looks on their faces. I reach for Mya and pull her close. Willow reaches out and tickles her tiny foot.

"Rece, she is so cute." Willow says.

Beaming. "I know." I kiss her on her forehead. "Hi, Mya, I'm your Uncle Rece." She smiles. My aunts are busy trying to get my mom situated on the sofa, as she tries to gain her composure. I am more than positive that she never imagined a Thanksgiving like this one is turning out to be. Dad decides to break the ice. "Well, I'll be hot damned! Now, this is what I call a Thanksgiving dinner!" He walks towards us. "Rece, let me see my first grandbaby! Well, aren't you just as cute as a button. I'm Papa!" He gently rocks Mya in his strong arms, and it's quite clear that he is a proud grandpa. Dad walks over to the couch, and my aunts all move so that he can sit next to my mom. "Ahhh Vikki, look at her. She's a little cutie." His voice softens. I'm glad his reaction is better than my mom's. At least it takes some of the sting out of how Bronson and Mindy must feel.

I'm proud of Willow because she doesn't get rattled at the sight of all of this craziness. She can hold her own. I like that.

Mom lifts her head, looks over at Mya, then at Willow, and back down at Mya, before jumping up and storming out of the room once again. This time she slams her bedroom door, and begins throwing things and cursing at the top of her lungs. After hearing the third glass object shatter against the wall, I decide to go check on her. Everyone is in shock…frozen. No one really knows what to do. Bronson and Mindy are hurt by Mom's outburst. Mindy starts crying and Bronson tries to comfort her. "Why does it matter that Mya is black? She's our baby and we love her?" Mindy manages to say through the tears.

"Babe, don't worry about Mom, she'll come around. Trust me." Bronson wraps his arm around her.

Dad stands, and hands the baby to Mindy, and says, "Listen up everyone. I know a lot has taken place today. Rece's engagement announcement and the welcoming of our new grandbaby. It's a lot to take in on one day, but it's a joyous time and we are going to have a wonderful Thanksgiving." Pausing slightly. "Rece and Bronson, go check on your mom." Looking towards my aunts, "Deb, will you ladies get everything in order so we can eat?"

"Sure thing, William." Deb replies, while shaking her head.

"And in keeping with the Gallantine tradition, we always ask one female guest to help me select the dinner wine, and one male guest to carve the turkey." Reaching for Mrs. James' hand. "Mina will you accompany me to the cellar to select a bottle?" He asks.

"Ummm, sure. I'd love to." Mrs. James looks over at Mr. James.

Dad senses that he may have overstepped his boundaries and backtracks. "Oh, Walter, is it okay with you if I steal your wife for a few minutes?"

"As long as you bring her back!" They all laugh.

"Sure thing, pal." My dad replies, before handing out more instructions. "Ladies, show Walter where we keep the official cutting knife, and Mina and I will be right back." My dad leads Mrs. James down a short flight of stairs to our cellar and I tell Willow that I'll return in a few minutes. Bronson and I head down the hall to check on our mother.

CHAPTER 45

We reach the bedroom and pause for a few seconds. Mom is still throwing things. Bronson slowly opens the ornate door and steps inside. I follow him. Once inside, we immediately take notice of the havoc Mom has wreaked on the once custom-decorated room. She has broken nearly all of her perfume bottles, and completely destroyed one of a kind figurine pieces she has collected over the years. The hand sewn Italian comforter that she waited six months for is cut to shreds. In one word, the room is a mess.

Mom is sitting on her lavender settee, staring out of the window as if her life has truly come to an end. Her makeup is smeared from the tears, and her coiffed hair has come undone. If we hadn't witnessed all of this mess, we would have thought a tornado blew through our parents' room.

"Mom, are you okay?" Bronson asks, while keeping a safe distance, in case Mom decides to throw anything else.

Mom doesn't utter a word.

I walk over to where she is sitting and kneel beside her. Grabbing one of her hands, I put my other arm around her waist and begin to lift her. "Come on, Mom, let's get you cleaned up. We have a very special dinner to attend."

Mom pushes my hands away, stands, and then darts a sharp look towards Bronson. "How could you do this to me?" Pointing at herself. "First Rece, then you! Do you guys hate me? Was I such a terrible mother?"

We realize that she's not really interested in hearing a response from either of us. She starts pacing the room. "All I've ever asked was that my sons marry, and give me some grandbabies.

Bronson interjects. "Mom, you do have a grandbaby. Mya is beautiful."

Mom raises her voice even louder. "Are you serious, Bronson? How am I supposed to deal with all of this shit? A black daughter-in-law, and a black grandchild? Really?"

"Mom, calm down." I say, in an effort to diffuse the situation.

"Shut up, Rece! All of this is your goddamn fault! Why couldn't you marry someone in our circle? Someone in our status? Damn it! You could have at least picked a light-skinned negro, or someone that could possibly pass, but noooooo; you had to have the dark chocolate one, didn't you? You're just like your goddamn father!" She storms forward and starts hitting me.

"Stop it, Mom! That's enough" Bronson yells, as he tries to step between us.

Mom has turned completely red, and I believe there's smoke coming from her nostrils. She has gone completely insane. I'm stunned, and I really don't know what to say to her right now. I grab both of her arms and toss her onto her bed.

"No, it's not enough! How will I ever explain this to my friends and family? I'll be the shame of Nashville! They'll disown me for sure!" She starts to cry, again.

I can't take this shit. "Mom, for crying out loud, this isn't about you. This is about me finding an incredible woman in this crazy, mixed up world. Someone that truly loves me for me, and not for the name. This is about Bronson and Mindy finally having a child of their own. Someone they can share their love with. It's not about you! I know that Dad has hurt you over the years, but you chose to stay. You chose lifestyle over love. Now, you have two choices, stay in this room and feel sorry for yourself because you're going to have a black daughter-in-law and a black grandchild, or clean yourself up and join the rest of the family in welcoming Willow and Mya into our family. At the end of the day, they are going to be a part of the family whether you like it or not. And for the record, I'm nothing like your goddamned husband!"

She gasps at my use of profanity. Bronson reaches out to touch her hand. "Mom, it's Thanksgiving. You're gonna have another great daughter-in-law and you're finally a grandmother. This is truly a blessing, Mom. Can't you see that?" Bronson pleads. He so wants her to embrace this moment.

"Ahhhh, get out! Both of you!" She yells, while throwing a pillow in our direction.

Bronson has had enough. "Fine, Mom! Be a bitch! But you will not ruin this moment for me and my wife. We are thrilled to be parents. Let's go, Rece." We storm out of the room.

Once in the hallway, I feel the need to comfort my little brother and try to lift his spirit. "Listen, Bronson, she doesn't mean any of this. She's just overwhelmed and filled with a whole lot of hurt. She'll come around. Just give her some time."

"Yeah, I hear you, Rece. I just don't understand how she can be so cold. Mya is beautiful. Anyone would be proud to be her grandmother."

Patting Bronson on the back. "She will be proud, just be patient, okay?"

Looking unconvinced. "Alright, if you say so."

"Have I ever been wrong, little bro?"

Bronson shoots me a smirk.

"Well." He replies.

I softly punch him in the arm and we embrace.

"Give me some." I say. Bronson and I bump fists and head back down the hallway to join the family.

The men are still gathered around the bar, and the women are in the dining room gushing over Mya. Willow looks up and blows me a kiss. I smile and feel the chill of the previous conversation with my mom exit quickly from my heart. *Willow's warmth.* I need a drink. I suppose my dad notices the tension and offers us a drink.

"Come on over here, sons. You both look like you could use a stiff one!" He laughs because he knows that Mom can be hard to handle at times.

"I think I'll take a double, Dad." Bronson replies, before sitting.

"A double it is." Dad says, while dropping two ice cubes into Bronson's glass. "How's your mom, Bron?"

"Ummm." Bronson begins.

"She'll be okay." I snap. I want to prevent Bronson from supplying my dad with any type of excuse for my mom's behavior.

"Yeah, she will." Dad replies. "Give her a few minutes." He knows her pattern far too well.

I grab my drink and walk over towards Mr. James. "How's everything going?"

"Everything is fine, Rece. How is your mom?"

"She'll be fine. Sometimes she can be a drama queen." I state, before taking a long sip of my aged whiskey.

Mr. James laughs. "Well, don't be so hard her. She's just a little taken aback. At least she didn't curse us out."

We both burst into laughter. "Point taken, sir."

My dad walks from behind the bar and addresses everyone. "Alright everyone, listen up. Give me a few minutes to get my lovely wife and we will officially start the Gallantine Thanksgiving dinner!" He pats his stomach before exiting the room.

CHAPTER 46

The warm, inviting scents of tarragon and sage has filled the air, and we are all anxiously waiting for my parents to return. The table is beautifully decorated with Mom's custom linens and our family china. Next to each place setting, Mom has chosen small, harvest pumpkins, filled with miniature ruby pomegranates, burnt orange tulips and gold roses. In the center of the table sits the masterpiece… the turkey. It is tastefully garnished with green muscadine vines and persimmons. I can't wait to devour the cornbread dressing with smoked bacon and pecans, along with Mom's famous mashed sweet potatoes. As always, Mrs. Victoria Gallantine knows how to entertain. I quickly reach down and grab one of the roasted parsnips, with a hint of mint, delicious. Willow catches me and taps me on the hand.

"Hey, you. Wait for your parents." She sweetly scolds.

"Oh, I forgot." I laugh. "I'm starving, I've been saving up for this all day."

"I bet you are starving." She whispers devilishly.

While no one is looking I tap her softly on the ass, and reply, "Yeah, I'm starving for that, too."

She starts to blush. "Rece, cut it out. We're at your parents' house."

"That makes it even better. Maybe we can sneak into my old room."

Willow tries to keep a serious, calm look on her face, as not to draw attention, but it doesn't work. I squeeze her hand as we both try to conceal our thoughts.

I glance over at Bronson and my heart warms at the sight of him placing soft kisses on Mya's cheeks. He and Mindy couldn't be happier.

My Aunt Friday opens the china cabinet, retrieves the official Gallantine turkey knife and fork, and hands them to Mr. James. She gives him a brief summary about the the Gallantine men and the special guests that have carved the Thanksgiving turkey prior to him. Mr. James is being the perfect gentleman by holding on to each word, and acting as if he's really interested. Aunt Friday loves the attention and becomes even more animated.

My Uncle Andy has made his way over to Mrs. James. She's giggling, which means he's probably telling her that she doesn't look old enough to have a daughter Willow's age. He's a real flirt once he's had a few drinks. My Aunt Zannavia is keeping her eyes fixed on his every move. She knows her husband quite well, and keeps his leash pretty damn tight.

In spite of all the drama, everyone seems to be enjoying themselves and still in the holiday spirit.

As promised, my dad returns with my mom. She looks gorgeous. She has changed into a stunning, strapless Givenchy sheath, in a lovely shade of pumpkin, trimmed with amazing jewels. Her makeup is really muted, and she's pulled her hair back into a bun. Her blue eyes still show a hint of tears, but she's pulled together. *Now that's my mom!*

My dad clears his throat. "May I have everyone's attention please? Victoria would like to say a few words before we eat." My dad leans down and kisses my mom on the cheek before stepping back and giving her the floor.

Mom takes a deep breath, and gently clasps her hands in front of her.

"First of all, I'd like to welcome each of you to our home. I want to sincerely apologize for my behavior earlier. This has been an overwhelming evening for all of us, I'm sure. First, learning of Rece's engagement, and then meeting my granddaughter for the first time. I'm sure that you all can understand that it is a great deal to try and digest on this family holiday." My aunts and uncles shake their heads in agreement. "My darling son, Rece, and his new fiancé, Willow. I am truly sorry. I hope that you can find it in your hearts to forgive me. Willow I look forward to getting to know you and your family."

Willow smiles.

"My baby boy, Bronson. Mommy loves you. Mindy you are the best. I'm so happy for the two of you, and incredibly happy about being a grandmother. Shit, if Angelina and Brad can have the entire human race, surely I can have a black…I mean, African American grandbaby." Mom walks towards Mindy and Bronson and reaches for Mya.

"Hi, Mya! Aren't you just the cutest. I'm your Mimi!" She pulls Mya close and kisses her on the forehead. "Oh, I can just eat you up. She is gorgeous!" Mom's face warms up and she begins to cry. This time it's tears of joy. "Again, my apologies to everyone. Now let's eat and enjoy all of these holiday blessings!"

We all join hands and my Uncle Frank prays for the families gathered and then blesses the food. It seems as if the holiday spirit has truly landed at the Gallantine home. *Now this is what I call a Thanksgiving dinner.*

"DESSERT"

CHAPTER 47

Mr. and Mrs. Walter James
request the pleasure of your company
at the marriage of their daughter
Willow Carol

to

Rece William Gallantine
son of Mr. and Mrs. William Gallantine
on Saturday, the twenty-fifth of December
two thousand and fourteen
six o'clock in the evening

Lowes Vanderbilt
2100 West End Avenue
Nashville, Tennessee

Black tie

I must be out of my freaking mind to have allowed Rece to convince me to get married on Christmas Day. Who plans a wedding in one month? No one! Well, I take that back. At least one crazy, insane individual in the entire universe, and that would be me!

Rece and I have tasted more cake samples than I care to remember. Almond, almond amaretto cream, chocolate, white chocolate raspberry, lemon, key lime, butterscotch walnut, pumpkin, rum, etc. Really? Well, I must admit, the white chocolate raspberry was off the chain. But seriously, it's really overkill because no matter what cake flavor we select, someone is going to complain. If we order beef, someone will complain that we didn't serve chicken. So, Rece and I are simply having the food items that we enjoy. If the guests love it, great! If not, oh well, life goes on.

I am extremely happy that the families agreed to keep the wedding small and intimate. After five tries, we finally narrowed the list down to one hundred and sixty people. It was tough, because Mrs. Gallantine wanted to invite every politician and socialite in the state of Tennessee. Rece quickly reminded his mom that this was our wedding, and we only wanted to invite people with whom we had a relationship. She pushed slightly, but realized that her son wasn't going to budge. So, one hundred and sixty people it is.

My parents have booked two ballrooms at Loews Vanderbilt Hotel to accommodate the wedding and reception. Rece and I really wanted something elegant. Neither of us like gaudy, so it's really important that everything, from the invitations to the favors, be tasteful.

I've visited New York twice looking for the perfect wedding dress and I finally settled on a beautiful, off-white

Pnina Tornai mermaid gown. The beading alone is beyond exquisite and it is repeated along my chapel train. I know that Rece is going to flip once he sees me in it.

We've opted for the traditional colors of black and white, with the colors of Christmas echoed throughout the decorations, bouquets, favors and invitations.

Journey and Mindy are my bridesmaids, and they'll be wearing long, strapless venetian red dresses with side ruching.

Rece's best men are Bronson and Devin. They will be sporting Georgio Armani tuxedos with velvet lapels. Their custom ties are being designed in Japan by a family friend of Rece's mom. I've seen some of the sketches, and the intricate embroidery showcase hints of Christmas evergreen and red. It's going to look amazing.

I just got off of the phone with my wedding planners Jennifer and Angelic of Wilson & Pendergrass, The Event Specialists. These women are known throughout the South as the eminent event planners. There's not a celebrity, or socialite, that hasn't used their services. They cost a pretty penny, but they are well worth it. I love the fact that they are two sharp, black sistahs doing their thing, and doing it well.

Jennifer and Angelic informed me that they were able to book a fabulous local singer by the name of Marci B, and that she'll be accompanied by members of the Nashville Symphony. Marci sings everything from jazz, to R&B, to Pop, so I am sure that everyone will enjoy her. I am so excited because she travels a lot and I was afraid she would be on the road. Yay! Things are falling into place.

I'm surprised that I am not stressed. A little anxious for everything to be over, but not stressed. I'm sure if I had six months to a year to plan this wedding I'd be a mess, but the time constraint is forcing me to stay on track. Rece and I haven't had much time together, but that's okay because we're both running around. We recently took some photos that we will give away as favors. Mrs. Gallantine is having them framed and engraved for each guest. I think it will add that personal touch we want.

I bought Rece a beautiful, diamond Concord watch for the big day. Journey is picking it up for me and I think he'll be pleasantly surprised.

In terms of work, I haven't seen one client. I was so sure that someone would curse me out when I announced I would be closed for eight weeks, but everyone gave their blessings. As off the chain as most of my clients are; they really are good people at heart. Also, it's not like I'm taking off for something foolish, I'm getting married!

After the ceremony, my honey and I are going to spend a month in Figi at the Tadrai Island Resort. No phones, no computers, no interruptions, just the two of us. It should be very romantic and relaxing. We'll be on a beachfront property, with our very own pool and butler. Who could ask for anything more?

As I'm setting some things aside to take on my fabulous trip, the phone rings. It's my girl, Journey.

"Hey, you!"

"Hey, girl…I mean, bride-to-be." She says with sass.

"You're so crazy! What's up, chick?"

"Nothing really. Mindy and I just finished our final fitting, and the dresses are gorgeous. I look pretty hot in mine. I'm gonna try and tone it down a bit, as not to steal all of your attention. Okay?" She laughs hysterically.

"Thank you, you are such a good friend." I reply.

"Shit, I know."

We both crack up.

"Crazy woman, did you pick up the watch?"

"Yes, I did. Chile you spent some bucks on this watch. It is nice!" Journey replies in her usual over-the-top way.

"Yeah, I did. It's for our big day; so I splurged."

"Well, baby, if ya'll ever split up I'm coming for the watch!"

"Journey, stop it!" Trying to control my laughter.

"Shit, if he breaks your heart…he gets nothing!"

Pausing for a moment to gain my composure. "Okay, little mama. I get it."

"Seriously, Willow, it's beautiful, and I love what you had engraved. You're such a romantic. Rece is gonna love it."

"I hope so."

"Don't worry, he will. By the way, Devin and I ran into Jordan last night at the Melting Pot." She says, as if she's waiting for a curt response.

"Really? Was he with Bambi?"

We both crack up.

"Naw, he was with some black professional networking group."

"Now that's funny. So, he's a black professional now?" I ask, dumbfounded.

"I guess so. You know he changes with the weather." Journey remarks.

"I know that's right."

"Well, I told him that you were getting married. I figured you wouldn't mind."

Goddamn it, Journey! You can't hold water."

"No, I don't mind." I lie.

"Shocked is an understatement of how he took the news. Brother man was blown away. I'm pretty sure I saw his eyes water up, but he acted as if he was really busy with his group and quickly got ghost. But, I could tell he was hurt. Oh well, serves his black ass right!" She states, with contempt.

"Journey, don't be mean. Jordan is a nice guy. He is immature, unfocused…but nice." I reply.

"That's for sure. I bet his ass will get focused now. Damn, it must hurt to lose to a white boy!" She lets out a robust laugh.

I sigh. "Journey, he didn't lose out to Rece. We just didn't work. At any rate, I'm glad that he knows. I wish I could have told him, but this is probably best. I don't have to deal with him explaining why we didn't work, or becoming angry. I really did love him, and we had some great times together. It just wasn't meant to be. Maybe he'll be good for someone else. Oh well, enough of that. Tell me about the dresses again." *I'm trying not to feel anything about Journey telling Jordan about my wedding, but there's a part of me that feels kind of sad. Not sad about our relationship ending, but about him as a person and his feelings. Even though we didn't work out, I still want him to be happy; because I know that beneath all of his junk, he loved me the best way he knew how.*

"They are awesome, and I looked HOT! So did Mindy!"

"Good for you. I'm glad you're pleased." I'm a little distracted by Journey's 411 report.

"What are you about to get into?" Journey inquires.

"I'm going to finish sorting through what I'm taking on my honeymoon, and then head over to my parents' for a minute."

"Okay, call me if you need anything."

"I will."

"Just think, in less than seventy-two hours you will be Mrs. Rece Gallantine."

I snap out of my slight daze at the thought. "I know, I can't believe it!"

"Believe it, sistah girl!"

"I probably won't see you until Saturday. Be on time, Journey." I firmly state.

"Who you talking to? You know how I roll." Chuckling.

"Yeah, I do. Be on time, heffa. I ain't playing with you." I reply, with a laugh.

"I will. Love ya' Willow."

"I love you, too."

CHAPTER 48

I'm sitting out on my balcony enjoying one of my favorite cigars, a Diplomaticos No. 2, along with a glass of Ron del Barrilito Three Star. I love how the hints of candied fruit in the rum play off of the nutty, medium-bodied cigar. This is truly becoming one of my favorite past times. I've become pretty good friends with Scott, the owner of the Cigar Lounge. He has really educated me on the different varieties of cigars, and what types of beverages compliment best. I thought I knew a little something, but after spending time in the lounge; and attending some of the smoking events, I can truly say that I was quite the novice. Now, when it comes to the art of cigar smoking; I am quickly learning the ropes.

Bronson and Devin asked me if I wanted to do the whole "bachelor party" thing, but I declined. Shit, I'm still recuperating from the plane ride. I really just needed a moment to myself. Ever since I convinced Willow to get married on Christmas Day, things have been absolutely bonkers. Not only are we planning a wedding, but we're building our dream home.

I took Willow to see the land my family has been saving for me and my future family. It's a gorgeous piece of property that sits in the heart of Brentwood, right off Concord Road. My plan is for our home to be the first built in the exclusive subdivision, The Willows. My future wife has no idea that I'll be building a subdivision in her honor. She will be thrilled.

We signed off on the architectural design, and met with the subcontractors to finalize some details. Our company will be overseeing the entire project, but I wanted a new set of eyes to assist with the building process. After meeting with several builders in this area, I decided to use a small, minority company owned by two brothers, Joshua and Jacob Wright. I attended a conference last year and they did a fantastic presentation on "green" building, and I knew then that I would use their services at some point. What better way than on my own home? Plus, it's really important for me to give back to the Nashville community, and assist others. Devin will also be working on this project, and getting a full introduction to the world of construction. I've already told him that this business is hard work, and if he wants to be successful he has to know every aspect. He says that he's on board. We'll see if he feels the same way after his first day of pouring concrete.

I take a long drag from my cigar, and enjoy the instant mellow feeling. Wow! I'm about to be a married man.

I wonder if I'll feel different once I take those ultimate vows? Will marriage be as wonderful as Bronson says, or a pain in the ass, as Dad says? Of course Dad would say that. I wonder if he ever truly loved Mom, or was his heart forever tied to someone that society wouldn't accept during those times? I'm pretty sure he cares about Mom, but they have always seemed disconnected on so many levels. I really feel sorry for her because she yearns to be loved, and I think if she didn't have my brother and I, she would have lived a depressed life.

At any rate, she has been a totally different person since Thanksgiving. She is so excited about the wedding, and her new grandbaby. It's been a joy to watch. She's even started back golfing. Willow mentioned that her dad saw Mom on the course last week, and shot a few rounds with her. I thought that was really nice of Mr. James, considering Dad will never set foot on a golf course. He says it's just not his thing. Oh well, I am glad that Mom is back doing some of the things she enjoys. I'm even happier that our families are really coming together as one.

At the end of the day, I believe that I've chosen the right woman for me and I believe our marriage will work.

Now, if for some unforeseen chance it doesn't; well it's been one hell of a ride! But, I know that it will. Nothing can stop us.

I'm just going to sit here and enjoy this significant moment. I take another sip of rum and notice two squirrels running across the yard.

Life is good.

CHAPTER 49

Somewhere, in the still of the night, two souls quietly slip out of bed, as not to disturb their partners, and quickly walk down dimly lit hallways. Once they have reached a space where they cannot be detected, they both reach in unison for their cell phones. One dials, while the other anxiously awaits the gentle vibration, indicating the anticipated voice on the other end.

"Hello."

"Hi, beautiful."

"Hi."

"I miss you."

"I miss you, more."

"When can I see you, again?"

"I'll see you at the wedding."

"I know, but what if I want to see you before then?"

"Uhhh, I don't know. We have to be careful."

"Yeah…I know, but I just can't stop thinking about you."

"Me, too."

"So, are we actually going to let this wedding take place?"

"I don't think we can stop it."

"But, what about us?"

"What do you mean?"

"I mean, what will we do about us?"

"I don't know. I just know that I haven't felt this wonderful in a long time."

"Me, too."

"Let's just take it one day at a time. Okay, love?"

"Okay."

"Darling?"

"Yes, love."

"I can still smell you."

"And, I can still taste you." Soft laughter.

"Good night."

"Sweet dreams."

CHAPTER 50

Twenty-four hours before the wedding

It's late in the afternoon and I am sitting on a bench in Centennial Park feeding ducks, while waiting on Rece to join me. Several mallards have gathered around my feet to retrieve the honey wheat bread I've brought for them. I love their dark green heads, black-curled tails, and yellow bills. After a few minutes pass, the female ducks join the feast. It's interesting that the female is light brown, with iridescent feathers and a brown bill as opposed to her dark-colored counterpart. I guess even in the animal world, females have to make their own fashion statement.

The weather is quite chilly today, so I made sure to layer and put on my heavy, grey wool overcoat. My feet are definitely warm because I'm wearing my Uggs. These are some of the ugliest boots I have ever seen, but they sure feel good on my feet. When Uggs first came out I thought, "White folks will wear anything." However, when Journey convinced me to try on a pair, I was sold and ready to climb the Alps. I couldn't believe boots could feel like heaven. I have been hooked ever since, and am now the proud owner of twelve pairs of Uggs.

I suppose I need to work on not saying white folks so much, since I am about to marry one. Rece always laughs when I tell him that he's acting white. He'll say something like, "Oh, you mean like when you're acting ghetto?" And my reply is always, "Who me? I don't ever act ghetto."

He'll give me a funny look and raise his brows before saying, "Really, babe? Come on, now. Only black people put ketchup on steak, and only black people carry hot sauce with them everywhere." We look at each other and always crack up, because he is sooooo right about ketchup and hot sauce.

That's the beauty of our relationship. We are able to appreciate our positives, and laugh at our shortcomings. As I reach for a few more slices of bread, I see Rece pulling up in his truck. It's covered in mud. He must have driven out to our new homesite. He steps out of his truck, wearing a black Norwegian sweater, with jeans and black alligator boots. He reaches back into his truck, and pulls out his favorite black, cowboy hat and places it on his head. I immediately start laughing because he knows that I love Tim McGraw, so he occasionally wears the same kind of black hat to play with me. Our eyes meet, and he starts laughing because he knows what I am thinking.

As he approaches the bench, I stand to greet him. We embrace and I allow my body to melt against his for a moment. He lifts my chin and kisses me softly.

"Hi, Tim." I greet him, jokingly.

He laughs, "Yeah, you wish."

We both chuckle at the thought.

I nudge him gently, and reply, "Naw, I'm happy with you, babe."

"You better be." Kissing me, again. "How are you?" He asks, as we both sit on the bench.

"Actually, I'm feeling pretty damn good!" I blush. "I'm not nervous, I'm not worried…I'm just at peace, and I can't wait to be Mrs. Rece Gallantine."

Rece grabs a few slices of bread and starts feeding the ducks. "Me, too, babe. I feel really good. I was thinking about us last night, and I must say I have never been so sure of anything in my life." Rece grabs my hand, and kisses my palm.

"Thanks, babe…that's sweet of you to say."

"I'm serious, Willow. I mean it…truly."

I grab the last slice of bread and break it into pieces before tossing it to the ducks. I scoot closer to Rece.

"Well, in less than twenty-four hours I will be your wife."

"Yep. I still can't believe that we managed to plan a wedding in less than a month. That's crazy. Who does that shit?" Rece rubs his hands together to remove some crumbs.

"Thank goodness for our mothers. Those two women are made for entertaining." I say.

"Yes, they are. It actually worked out, because it really took the majority of the stress off of us." Rece puts his arm around me.

"That's so true. I think the most stressful part was narrowing down the guest list and finding a dress."

"Yeah, it's been pretty smooth. Jennifer and Angelic have been on top of every detail. I'm glad we went with them." He says.

"Me, too. They're the best." I reply, as I stroke Rece's thigh.

Rece leans in and nibbles my ear. I giggle. "I miss our time together." He says.

"Me, too. But, you do agree that it was a good decision to chill on sex before the wedding, right?"

"Hell no!" Rece laughs, and then pats my leg. "Just kidding. I think it was a good idea. Plus, I am still floating from the plane ride. But, I still miss holding you at night."

I let my head rest on his shoulders. "Well, in less than twenty-four hours, you'll be holding me every night, for the rest of our lives."

"I can live with that." Rece replies, before kissing the top of my head.

"You better." I say, before sitting up straight and facing Rece.

"On another note, how are your parents? I know they have been busy trying to make everything perfect for their baby girl."

"I stopped by their place a few days ago, and Mom was in the zone making sure everything is in order. She seemed a bit preoccupied…maybe it's all of the wedding stuff." I pause slightly as I ponder my mom's mood a few days earlier. "Dad was golfing as usual. Mom says that he thinks he's the senior version of Tiger Woods. I guess he's just enjoying having some free time. He works so hard, and he finally decided not to take another contract out of the country for a while. I'm glad he's slowing down. Maybe now he and Mom will spend more time together.

"I'm sure that would be nice." Rece chimes.

"Yeah, because Dad retired Mom when she turned 50, so she has been solo for some time now."

"Does your mom golf?"

"A little, but I don't think she really cares for the sport."

"Well, maybe my mom can convince her to get back on the course, again."

"That'll be pretty hard, but we'll see. She needs to get out more. I suppose she has always just made sure that my dad was taken care of, and she really didn't want anything to interfere with that. Who knows?" For some strange reason I realize that my mom really does very little for herself. Maybe after the wedding, she will spend more time with your mom and become more social.

Rece removes his hat and runs his fingers through his hair. "I saw my parents earlier today. Dad was watching a marathon of *Law & Order* and Mom had just finished meeting with her stylist, and was headed to the golf course. She finally selected her gown for the wedding, so she was on cloud nine. Of course, she was asking me a thousand things. "Rece, have you taken care of this? Rece, do you know who is handling that?" I just finally told her to chill and that everything will get done. She is so excited. It's been a long time since I've seen my mom this happy." He smiles at the thought. I can see how much he really loves his mom.

I reach for his hand. "Well, babe, are you ready?"

"Ready as I'll ever be."

"Are you all packed?" I ask.

"Not quite. Shit, I plan on being butt-naked the whole honeymoon."

"You so nasty, Rece." I say, before he pulls me closer to him and slides his hand under my coat to tease my honey bunny. I giggle and squirm with delight.

I nudge him. "You better stop it before we get arrested."

He laughs and whispers, "I miss it."

"It misses you more." We laugh, again, at our obvious giddy behavior.

"Alrighty then." Rece stands and lifts me to join him.

"You ready?" He asks.

"Been ready!"

"Well, I can't wait to see you in your dress. Still no clue?" Rece asks.

"Nope." I say, while motioning that my lips are sealed.

"Okay." Rece says, looking disappointed.

"You'll have to wait just like everyone else." I say, slyly.

"Cool. Oh, I forgot to tell you that the ties came in today. They really look nice. Mom's friend did an excellent job."

"That's great, because I was a little nervous about how she was going to incorporate the traditional Christmas colors, but once I saw the sketches, I knew they would be sharp."

"They are."

"I talked to Mindy and Journey, and they both picked up their dresses yesterday. So, everything is in place."

Rece grabs both my hands and looks me in the eyes, "My beautiful wife-to-be, I guess I will be seeing you tomorrow night, six o'clock sharp."

I begin to cry, and Rece brushes the tears from my face and says, "I know...me, too."

"I love you so much, Rece." I lean into his chest and wrap my arms around his waist.

We embrace in silence...taking in the magnitude of the moment. We realize that in this huge world, where people spend very little time cultivating true relationships and longing for microwave love, we were able to find each other and create a beautiful bond. One based on true friendship and authentic love. Call it luck…call it fate…we call it blessed…truly blessed.

CHAPTER 51

The Wedding Day...Groom's Suite

It's official! In less than an hour, I will be a married man. This is great! I didn't get an ounce of sleep last night. I suppose I was too anxious about today. Willow called around midnight and we stayed on the phone until nearly two in the morning, reminiscing about our courtship. Neither of us could have imagined that a trip to Cracker Barrel would result in marriage. It's kind of funny when you actually think about it. Maybe we will make it a monthly ritual once we're man and wife.

I finish putting on my cuff links and slip on my Ferragamo oxfords I bought especially for today. _Nice._ As I am reaching for my tie, I hear a knock at the door. It's Bronson and Devin. They look sharp.

"Hey, man, you ready?' Devin asks, before giving me some dap and a hug.

"I'm almost ready. I have to put on my tie, and then I'll be set. I hope I look as tight as you guys." I reply, as I place my tie around my neck.

"I doubt it, but you can try." Bronson jokes, as he nudges me in the arm and immediately starts assisting me. I give him a sharp, playful look.

"How are you feeling today, bro?" Bronson asks with a smile.

"I couldn't be better." I reply

"Now, that's what I want to hear." Bronson says, while looping my tie into a Double Windsor.

"I have to admit, I am a little nervous. But I guess that's to be expected. I just want to see my lady walking down the aisle." I smile at the thought.

Bronson tightens my tie, and pats me on the shoulders. "There, now you're all set, big brother."

I step closer to the full length mirror to examine Bronson's work. "Good job, little brother. I believe I taught you well." I laugh.

"Yeah, yeah take all of the credit. I am who I am because of you." Bronson replies, sarcastically.

I give him a playful stare and say, "Well, now...you might be right." Bronson shakes his head in disbelief, and then bursts into laughter.

Devin has been busy over at the bar pouring us shots of Patron. He picks up all three shot glasses and walks towards us. "Here, guys." We each take a glass.

Devin clears his throat, as if he about to make a grand announcement. He can be quite amusing at times. "Rece, you're about to marry a wonderful woman. I hope that you and Willow grow old together, and have a life filled with lots of joy and happiness. You guys deserve this. Cheers!"

In unison, we all say, "Cheers!" before extending our glasses, toasting and downing the smooth tequila.

"Whew, I think that's what I needed to get the nerves out." I say, while making the standard ugly face that all men make after they take a shot. Devin coughs, Bronson pats his chest and I walk around for a few seconds waiting for the burning sensation to stop. We all laugh at ourselves. I am sure we are thinking, "Why in the hell do we do this shit?" Oh well, its man thing.

There's another knock at the door. It's Jennifer, one of our wedding coordinators. She's an attractive, black woman. Kind of on the curvy side, and sports a shoulder length blonde bob. Not every black woman can get away with being blonde, but Jennifer does a hell of a good job at it.

"Hey, guys! Mmmm, ya'll look good." She says, while placing a box of boutonnieres on the bed, along with her leather tote bag. Jennifer walks towards Devin and straightens his tie. "There you go, now you're straight." She says, coyly, and winks. Devin coughs out of nervousness, and politely thanks her. She laughs at his obvious discomfort.

"Oh, before I forget." Jennifer reaches into her tote, pulls out a small box and hands it to me. "It's from Willow!" She says, with an air of excitement in her voice.

I look at the box and smile. Jennifer softly punches me on the arm. "Come on, open it! What are you waiting for?" I sit on the side of the bed and slowly remove the red and green decorative paper. I lift the lid of the stainless steel box with my initials deeply engraved and am pleasantly surprised. It's a stunning white diamond, Concord watch. It's beautiful.

"Ahhh, man, she must really love you, dog." Devin says, as everyone shakes their head in agreement.

I smile, because I know that she truly does love me.

"Read the back!" Jennifer says with great enthusiasm

I flip the watch over and instantly feel myself begin to blush.

Time stands still
When I am in your arms
Willow

I show Bronson and Devin. "That's really nice." Bronson says, as he takes a closer look at the exquisite timepiece.

"By the way, my partner, Angelic, is taking your gift up to Willow as we speak."

"Ahh, okay…cool. Thanks." I reply, not really listening because I'm in a zone.

Jennifer pins a boutonniere on each our lapels, and quickly grabs her things. "I'll be back in exactly twenty minutes. All of your guests have arrived, and everything looks amazing. Now, just relax until I return." Jennifer gives me a hug, winks at Devin once more, and dashes out the door to check on Willow and her bridesmaids.

I slip my watch on and take one last look at myself as a single man. *This is it man! This is it!*

The Wedding Day...Bride's Suite

It took nearly three hours for my beautician, Rolonda, to finish my hair. She was adamant that my hair be perfect on my wedding day, and so she took her sweet time pinning each strand into its rightful place. The smell of Pink Oil Lotion, hair gel and curling irons linger in the air. These are the essential products needed in order to create the perfect Audrey Hepburn updo. When Rolonda handed me the mirror to check out my bridal hair, I was blown away. It was all I imagined and more.

Now, I'm in the hands of my makeup artist, Kyra. I met Kyra a few years ago at a women's convention in Las Vegas. She had a booth where she performed live makeovers. She was incredible. To see her transform someone's look from boring to dazzling was just amazing. We exchanged business cards and quickly became friends. She offered to do the makeup for my entire bridal party as a wedding gift. I insisted that I pay her something, but she refused. I adore her.

"Okay, Willow, don't move." Kyra gently demands, as she applies the last false eyelash. "Just one more sec...don't open your eyes." Kyra turns my chair around to face the mirror. "Okay, you can open your eyes now."

The image I see of myself is just breathtaking. I imagined that I would be a pretty bride, but I never imagined this. "Oh my God! Ohhh... I... uhhh, Kyra, this is perfect!" I say, before my eyes start to tear up. Everyone in the room is smiling. My mom immediately starts to cry. "My baby! You look so beautiful." Mom leans down, and kisses me on the cheek.

"Kyra, I can't thank you enough. You really did a fabulous job." I say, while still staring at myself in disbelief.

"Girl, it's easy to do makeup when you have a great canvas." She winks at me and quickly begins to dab at my eyes as not to disturb my makeup. "Oh, no, you don't! Not after all of this hard work baby." She states with a firm tone.

I look at my mom, again, and she is bawling. "Mommy, don't cry." I say.

"I know, baby. It's just that you're all grown up now, and I am so happy for you." She reaches for my hands and squeezes them tightly, before whispering in my ear. "Willow, remember to always honor you…never, ever, settle for second place. Okay? Promise me." Mom looks at me in a way that I've never seen before. For the first time in my life I see sadness in her eyes. I'm concerned.

"I promise, Mom. Are you sure you're okay?" I ask with care.

She pats my hand. "I'm fine, baby, Mommy is fine."

"I love you, Mom."

"I love you more. Now, let me go sit over here and let Kyra fix me up. The mother of the bride can't be looking shabby." She laughs.

"Mrs. Williams, there is nothing shabby about you." Kyra replies.

"Baby, you are too kind." Mom says, before sitting down in the chair near the window, and letting Kyra work her magic.

Mindy and Journey are both smiling at me. They look so pretty in their gowns. The rich red looks good on them both. "Willow, Rece is going to flip when he sees you walking down the aisle." Mindy says.

"Yeah, girl, you are a fabulous bride…but, I knew you would be." Journey says, while removing my wedding gown from the opaque garment bag. "Come on…it's time for you to get dressed."

I take one last glance at my makeup, and remove my robe. I feel the butterflies erupt as I step into my gown. Mindy zips me and fastens each delicate button, while Journey assists me with my red, Jimmy Choo pumps.

"Aren't they hot?" I ask Journey.

She replies, "Fire, baby…fire!"

We laugh. Mindy looks at us with a bewildered look, and we both crack up, again, because we realize that she has no clue as to what we are talking about.

Journey tries to compose herself. "Mindy, when we say that something is fire, we simply mean that it's hot…it's to die for."

Mindy laughs. "Ohhh. I get it now. I thought I was going to have to call the fire department."

We all die laughing and Journey just shakes her head in disbelief.

"Stop it, you guys, I can't take much more. Mindy you are too funny! Seriously, I'm about to get married and I need my composure." As I gather myself, Journey places my tiara and veil on my head. Once in place, I take a few steps towards the full- length mirror, and can't help but smile. I keep telling myself not to cry, because I don't want to mess up my makeup…but, I will never forget this moment. My Pnina Tornai gown looks even more beautiful today. I love the form fit and exquisite beading. It's the perfect dress for me. I turn towards my mom, and she gives me two thumbs up and smiles. Kyra is doing a fabulous job on Mom, too.

Suddenly, I am startled by a knock at the door. Mindy opens it and there stands Angelic.

"Ohhh, Willow! Wow! Wow! You are doing this thang, baby!" Angelic is carrying a large box which she places on the bed, along with her purse. She gives me a soft hug.

"Thanks, Angelic."

"Well, I just wanted everyone to know that all of the guests have arrived, and we will begin the ceremony shortly." Angelic removes the lid from the large box. "Here are your bouquets. Aren't they beautiful?" She hands everyone their flowers.

"They are. I love them!" I reply with glee, as I examine my bouquet of white roses and pearls.

"Okay, I will be back in exactly fifteen minutes." Angelic grabs her bag, and heads for the door. "Oh, I almost forgot!" She reaches into her pocket and pulls out a small box. "This is for you, Miss Willow. It's from Mr. Gallantine." She smiles and places the tiny, decorated box in my hand. I feel myself begin to blush. *What has Rece gone and done now?*

"I'll see you guys in a few minutes." Angelic dashes out the door.

I take a few steps, and sit on the edge of the bed to open my gift from Rece. First, I read the small card attached.

Your something new…always, Rece

I remove the wrapping and smile when I see the Tiffany box. I open it to reveal a stunning pair of Tiffany Legacy diamond earrings. I gasp.

"Wow! Rece is doing it up, girl! Journey says.

"They are gorgeous, Willow." Mindy concurs.

My mom walks over to where I am sitting. "Let me help you." She says as she removes the earrings from the box, and places one in each ear. "These are very nice. Now, you're almost ready." Mom reaches over into her purse and pulls out a light blue, silk handkerchief and places it in my hand. "This belonged to your great-grandmother, Sweetie Alice, then my mother, Zora, and she passed it along to me…and now, I'm giving it to you…my darling, precious daughter. I hope you pass it on to your daughter. You are my heart." She begins to cry. I wipe her tears, and she pecks me on the lips.

"Thank you, Mom. This means so much." I stand and we embrace. By now the entire room is crying.

"Okay, everyone, we have got to stop this. Today is a happy day! Let's get ourselves together, because we have a wedding to attend!" Journey shouts.

"Amen!" Mindy replies.

Kyra grabs her tools, and begins touching up everyone's makeup. Within a few minutes, Angelic is back at the door to lead us all downstairs. I take a deep breath and simply say, "Thank you, Lord."

The Ceremony

The grand ballroom doors are about to open. My stomach is doing flips. I squeeze my dad's hand, really hard. He lifts my chin and looks into my eyes, "I couldn't be a prouder father. I love you, baby girl," he says, before wiping a tear from his face.

"I love you, too, Daddy, but you'll always be my favorite guy." I smile, and Dad kisses me on the cheek. He places my hand through his arm and says, "Are you ready?"

I quickly reply, "Yes, sir! Very."

The ushers open the doors, and I can see Rece and our bridal party. I am immediately struck with a flood of emotion, and I can't control my tears. *Damn it! I don't want to mess up my makeup. Oh well…too late for that.*

The room is more than I ever imagined. When I told Jennifer and Angelic that I wanted a "Winter Wonderland", I imagined something simple…yet, elegant. But, they have truly transformed this entire space into something out of the movies.

Snow flocked firs, with white lights, accented with red, green and gold decorations, surround the room. Large, crystal Christmas balls, icicles and snowflakes are hanging from the ceiling. Each crystal ball has the same coordinating, velvet ribbon as the trees, along with gold-tipped pine cones, red berries, poinsettias and greenery. Behind the custom-built altar, stands another twenty-foot, Frasier Fir. The tree is decorated with larger versions of the decorations gracing the smaller trees. There are thousands of white lights, and artificial, snow-covered mountains, that have made anyone sitting in this space feel as if they are actually sitting in a "Winter Wonderland". It is breathtaking, to say the least. I am truly taken aback.

The band begins to play Adele's *Lovesong*, the guest all stand, and Marci begins to sing. Everyone is smiling, as Dad and I, take our journey down the aisle. Rece and I lock eyes, and he begins to cry. As I get closer to Rece, I notice my mom on the left, and Mr. and Mrs. Gallantine to my right. They look really good. Both of our moms could give someone a run for their money on the red carpet. They really are two beautiful women. I hope I age as graceful as they have. Mom throws me a kiss, and I smile.

We make it to the altar and Dad kisses me, again, before turning and shaking Rece's hand. They embrace... Afterwards, Dad takes my hand and places it in Rece's before taking his place next to Mom.

The bridal party is all smiles. Journey winks.

Rece whispers, "You look gorgeous."

"Not too bad yourself, handsome." I chuckle, before turning towards Pastor Brownlow.

"You may all be seated. Dearly Beloved, we are gathered here today in the presence of God, and these witnesses, to join Willow Carol and Rece William, in holy matrimony. Marriage is sacred, and should not be entered into unadvisedly. If any person can show just cause as to why they may not be joined, let them speak now, or forever hold their peace."

Pastor Brownlow looks around the room, to ensure that no one is opposed.

"Rece and Willow have written their own vows." Pastor Brownlow gives me a nod and hands me the microphone.

"Rece, thank you. Thank you for loving me completely, and unselfishly. I always dreamed that I would meet someone as wonderful as my dad, and then you came along. You've made me realize that dreams do come true. You are truly the ultimate love of my life. I thank God that you found me. I pledge my love to you, today, tomorrow and always."

I give the mic to Rece and he proceeds to grab both of my hands. "Willow, thank you. Thank you for loving me completely and unselfishly. I never knew what I really wanted, or needed, until I met you. You've made me a believer of true love. I thank God for you, and I pray that

God allows me to continue to be the man designed for you. You are my one love…today, tomorrow and always."

"Who supports this couple in their marriage?" Pastor Brownlow asks.

Our parents stand and say in unison, "We do."

"May I have the rings?"

Bronson reaches into his pocket, and hands a diamond, platinum band to the pastor and Journey follows suit.

Pastor Brownlow places his bible on the stand near him, and holds both rings up so that everyone can see them. "These rings represent the two of you becoming one in every aspect of your life. Rece, repeat after me. I, Rece William Gallantine, give you, Willow Carol, this ring as a symbol of my unwavering love."

Rece repeats the vow, while lovingly gazing into my eyes.

"Willow, repeat after me. I, Willow Carol, give you, Rece William Gallantine this ring as a symbol of my unwavering love."

I repeat the vow, and feel myself begin to blush.

"By the power vested in me, by the State of Tennessee, I now pronounce you husband and wife. Rece, you may kiss you wife."

"Finally!" Rece says, excitedly. He grabs my face gently, and we share the most delicate kiss ever.

Pastor Brownlow laughs, and then announces, "Ladies and gentlemen, I present to you, Mr. and Mrs. Rece Gallantine!"

Everyone stands and applauds, as Rece and I, make our way toward the doors. We are showered with rose petals, as our bridal party follows us into the hallway. Once outside the doors, Rece and I embrace, and squeeze in another kiss.

"Well, babe, we did it!"

"I know, honey. I am so happy, Rece!"

"Me, too, babe. It's the best day of my life."

Before we have a chance to wallow in our bliss, we are bombarded by family and friends. However, after a few minutes go by, Angelic squeezes through the crowd and informs us that the ushers are going to start directing the guests into the reception area. She also tells us that the photographer will be ready shortly. We thank Angelic for all of her hard work and we then see our parents making their way through the crowd. Rece's mother gives us both a huge hug and kiss, before bragging about the ceremony. "This was just absolutely fabulous. This wedding will be the talk of Nashville. Mark my words, darling." She gleams with pride.

Mr. Gallantine leans down, and kisses me on the cheek. "You look beautiful, love. Congratulations!"

"Thank you, Mr. Gallantine."

He extends his hand to Rece. "Son, you've done good."

"Thanks, Dad."

"Willow, you were a stunning bride." Mrs. Gallantine says, in her molasses tone.

"That she certainly was." My mom says, as she walks up. "Hi, baby."

"Hi, Mom." We hug, and Dad gives me a peck on the lips.

Everyone is so happy. It is incredibly heartfelt to feel such love. I can't wait for our first dinner party. This time, it will really be a family gathering. We stand around and give a few more hugs, and partake in small talk. Mrs. Gallantine tells the immediate family that they should go and greet some of the guests before the reception officially starts. Everyone agrees, and they each jet off. Jennifer taps me on the shoulder, and says that we have about thirty or so minutes before pictures. She suggests we go up to the wedding suite to get a little quiet time and to freshen up.

"That sounds good to me." Rece says.

"Okay, but hurry back." Jennifer hands us the room key, and we head towards the elevators.

"Where are ya'll going?" Asks Journey, and the rest of the gang. We turn towards her, and begin to laugh because she has this funny look on her face.

"Girl, we're going up to the wedding suite to freshen up before pictures." I reply.

Journey is still looking at us, as if we're up to something. "Ummm, okay…cool. But bring ya'll asses right back here. Don't be trying to sneak off!" She starts cracking up.

"We promise, crazy woman." Rece says, before grabbing my hand and scurrying off to catch the elevator.

CHAPTER 52

Willow and I dash off the elevator in hopes of stealing a few sexy moments before taking pictures, and heading to the reception. I remove the key card from my pocket and swipe it, but it doesn't work. So, I try again, but the door still won't open. Willow takes the card from my hand, and looks down at the numbers brightly displayed, and begins to chuckle.

"Honey, this is the wrong room." She shakes her head. "Lord, please help my husband."

My heart warms instantly from hearing Willow say the word husband. I look at the card, and can't help but laugh at my oversight. "My bad."

Willow takes a few steps to the right. "Here is it," motioning me to follow, "room 305 is over here, darling."

I follow her and she decides that she'll swipe the card this time, and just like clockwork, the door opens. We can't get inside the room fast enough. I immediately pull Willow close to me. She wraps her arms around my neck, as I grab her ass and thrust against her. She pants in delight. We kiss…hard…deep…passionately. Our bodies are yearning to get out of these clothes and fuck, but we know it's not an option. At least not for now. So, we slowly grind and enjoy the temporary moment of heat.

I feel Willow's hand on my crouch, and I moan.

"I can't wait until tonight." She whispers in my ear. The heat of her breath sends a chill through me.

"I can't wait, either." I sigh with long awaited anticipation.

We make our way around the corner, and fall gently onto the large, comfy sofa. My hands continue exploring my wife's ass, and out of instinct and utter, fucking horniness, I lift her dress and begin spreading her thighs.

Suddenly, we are both startled by noises coming from down the hallway. Willow and I instantly stop what we're doing, and jump up from the couch. "What the hell is that, Rece?" Willow asks, in shock.

"I don't know, babe, but we're about to find out." I grab Willow's hand and head down the hallway. The sounds are becoming more audible as we approach the first room. We are in shock, because we realize that we have literally walked in on someone's love making session. But, who? The room is reserved under our name.

"Oh, baby, fuck me...fuck me harder!"

"Yeah baby, give me this pussy!"

"I want to feel all of your black cock inside of me!"

"Is that what you want? Huh? Tell me, again!"

"Oh yeah, Walter, fuck this white pussy, Daddy!"

When Willow hears her dad's name, she immediately grabs the handle and pushes the door wide open. What we are witnessing is beyond anything either of us could have imagined. All I can see is the back of Mr. James and my mom's pale white legs, spread eagle. "Daddy! What are you doing?" Willow screams.

"Mom, what the fuck?" I yell.

Mr. James jumps up and scrambles to find his pants, while my mom hurries to pull her dress down.

Willow charges at her dad. "How could you do this to Mommy? How could you Daddy?" She shouts, while fiercely hitting him. I grab Willow and pull her away from her dad. She bursts into tears.

My mom reaches out to touch Willow.

"Oh, Willow, darling, I'm so sorry. I never meant…"

Before she can touch Willow's arm, I push my arm out in front to prevent her from getting near Willow. "You never meant what, Mom? Never meant to fall on Mr. James' dick? Never meant to to get caught? What? What?" I ask, not really expecting an answer that will excuse this moment.

Mom tries to calm me down. "Rece, baby, listen to me." She says, while reaching for my arm. I quickly snatch it away. "Don't touch me, Mom! This is so fucked up!"

"Alright, son, don't talk to your mom that way." Mr. James firmly interjects.

I shoot him a look that he'll never forget, and begin to step towards him before Willow tightly grabs hold of my arm. "Mr. James, with all due respect, you are in no position to tell me how to talk to my mom."

Willow dries her eyes, and just looks at her dad. I've never seen this kind of pain in her eyes. "Daddy, I just don't understand. Wasn't Mom good enough? I mean, why her of all people? This is so wrong. I'll never forgive you for this, Daddy…never!"

Mr. James starts walking towards Willow, but she runs out of the room. "Willow, baby, let me explain!" He yells.

I give Mom and Mr. James another look of disdain, before taking off after Willow.

Neither of us get very far, because when Willow opens the hotel door she is met by our entire wedding party...including Dad, and Mrs. James. Willow is crying uncontrollably, so everyone knows that something is wrong. To add insult to injury, Mom and Mr. James come running around the corner trying to catch us.

Dead silence.

Everyone's eyes are on us.

Willow runs to her mom, and falls into her arms. "Oh, Mommy, how could he do this to you?"

Mrs. James pats Willow on the back softly, and tries to console her. "Oh, baby girl, don't cry. I'm okay. Please don't cry, it's your wedding day, you should be smiling, not crying. This has absolutely nothing to do with you okay." She begins wiping away Willow's tears, but Willow pushes her away.

"What are you talking about, Mom? You know about Daddy and Mrs. Gallantine?"

Very calmly, and without much emotion Mrs. James replies, "Yes, baby. I've known for quite some time, now."

Everyone gasps at Mrs. James' response, and all eyes turn toward my dad. He steps into the room and stands just a few inches behind me.

"Victoria, what the hell is going on?" He angrily asks.

Mom doesn't say a word, but instead inches closer towards Mr. James. By now, my dad has turned tomato red, and before I know it, he rushes pass me and grabs Mom by the neck. "You bitch---you fucking bitch!" Dad is infuriated.

Mr. James tries to intervene, but Dad catches him with a good left punch that sends him plummeting to the floor.

I grab my dad and try to restrain him. "Calm down, Dad!" He jerks away from me, and begins pacing the floor.

"Calm down! How the fuck can I calm down when my wife is up here fucking a goddamn nig…" He catches himself and stops mid-sentence.

"Say it, William!" My mom yells. "Say it!" She boldly walks up to my dad. "I was up here fucking a nigger, and you can't take it!" She laughs a sinister laugh. "All of these years, I've sat around and let you screw one black woman after the next. All while I sat at home. Well, not anymore. I've got me a taste of some nigger dick, and you know what they say, 'Once you go black, you won't go back.'" She laughs again and Dad spits in her face. "You cunt!" He says, before quickly exiting the room, and pushing past the bridal party. My uncles try to stop him, but he brushes them off.

This is truly a Kodak moment. The look on everyone's face is utter disbelief. No one says a word.

"This is my fucking wedding day! How does this kind of shit happen on my big day? Can anyone here explain to me why this is happening?" Willow starts crying, again. I feel like crying, too. This is too much for anyone to fathom. I grab Willow by the arm and turn to exit the the room.

My mom begins to speak. "Listen up, I need everyone to take a deep breath, and calm down. I apologize. I realize that this is a huge shock for everyone. I was really hoping that Walter and I would be able to break this news to everyone under different circumstances…but, oh well…the cat's out of the bag. I am going to freshen up, and I suggest that each of you do the same. We have a lovely reception to attend, and nearly two hundred guests to greet." My mom says, as if what just happened is insignificant.

"What?" I am in awe. "Mom, are you out of your mind? We aren't going to the reception. How can we go to a reception at a moment like this?" I grab Willow's hand and walk out of the room. My mom runs to the door and pushes her way through the crowd.

"Rece William Gallantine, get back here, right now!"

I pause and turn to look at my mom. She walks up to me and grabs my arm.

"Now you listen to me. You are a Gallantine! Do you hear me? A Gallantine! I know that this is a difficult moment, but we have close to two hundred people downstairs. Some of the biggest dignitaries in Tennessee are waiting on us. So, we're going to go downstairs and smile, eat our lovely dinner and dance the night away. It's not the end of the world---I just fucked someone, and got caught! Now suck it up!"

Willow squeezes my hand and with her free hand wails off and slaps my mom into oblivion. Leaving a distinct hand print across her face. "Fuck you, and fuck a goddamn reception. We're outta here!"

Mom screams, "Rece! Your wife just hit me! Aren't you gonna say something?"

"No, Mom…not a thing!" Willow and I apologize to the wedding party, and catch the next elevator. Once inside, we hold each other tight, and without saying a word we realize that our lives have been profoundly and tragically changed, in more ways than one. How will we ever recover from this?

Chapter 53

Somewhere in the dark of the night, two familiar souls connect in a smoke-filled blues bar in downtown Nashville. As the singer belts out a tune about why her baby done left her…these intrinsically bound souls find comfort, while sharing a bottle of wine. They laugh at the recent discovery of the affair, but agree that their marriages were over long before tonight's dreadful unearthing.

They toast! As their glasses tap, they smile and their eyes connect. Neither says a word, but slowly reaches out across the worn, wooden table and grab hands. The electricity felt is undeniable, and the quiet storm that they kept buried in the tiny corners of their hearts is about to roar.

Without saying a word, he pays the tab and gives a nod that they should go. This time, there are no uncles nudging him on, or a father insisting that it's time that he became a man. Today, he is a man…a full-grown man that has never gotten over his first, forbidden love. He could hardly contain himself when she walked through his front door on Thanksgiving Day. "Could this actually be her?" He thought to himself. That's why he insisted that she help him select the dinner wine. It wasn't until they were at the bottom of the stairs, that he leaned in closer, and got a hint of her scent. She smelled the same...like warm, sugar cookies straight from the oven.

When she reached between his legs, gently caressed his nature, and softly hummed that bluesy tune he could never get out of his head...he knew it was her...Wilhelmina "Helen" Brooks.

Now, some thirty-plus years later, their lives are woven once again through the marriage of their children, and the adultery of their spouses.

They quickly exit the bar to reinvent that moment of passion...if only for one night.

CHAPTER 54

It has been nearly a month since my wedding disaster, and I still can't believe what happened. My dad fucking Mrs. Gallantine! I mean, what kinda shit is that? But, what burns my butt most is that Mom knew, and didn't say one solitary thing to me about it. This is the type of drama that takes place on television, not in real life.

My husband and I cancelled our honeymoon, because things were just crazy after the ceremony. Both of our fathers moved out, and no one is speaking. It's truly a hot mess. I haven't been able to wrap my mind around any of this, and so I have just retreated. Our bedroom has become my sanctuary to wallow in sadness. Rece says that I need to snap out of it, and just accept that shit happens. I completely understand his position, and I also know that in order for him to go on with his life, he needs to remove all emotion. It's not that easy for me.

I thought my parents had the perfect marriage. They were so in love. Or, at least I thought so. If my parents' marriage is falling apart, then there is no hope for me and Rece. *Stop it, Willow. You and Rece will be fine.*

Speaking of my husband, he's out of town for several days on family business, so I am completely on my own.

My girl, Journey, has been calling me every day, but I really haven't felt like dealing with anyone. Mommy and Daddy have left several messages as well, but for right now, I just need a little space. Space from work…space from family…space from friends…space from the world. To be perfectly honest, I'm just stressed and I need some relief. I wish I could take a pill and make this whole ordeal magically disappear, but that's not going to happen.

I need to get out of bed and get dressed. I promised Rece that I would go and check on our house while he was away. He's been gone for three days, and I haven't moved. *What the hell!* Let me jump in the shower and drive over to our future residence. But, first, I'm gonna have me a nice, tall glass of wine. *Damn, girl it ain't even noon, yet. Oh well, I need a drink.*

As I am driving down Old Hickory Boulevard, it dawns on me that this will be my driving route from now on. I like this area of Brentwood. It's far enough from the city to have a somewhat country feel, but offers excellent access to shopping and restaurants. I think we're going to enjoy our new life, in our new home.

I make a quick left onto Franklin Road, and I can see our spectacular 20,000 square foot, French chateau. It's breathtaking. I pull slowly into our private driveway, and am excited to see the landscaping nearly complete. Rece will be thrilled.

There are two Ford F-150's parked in the driveway, so I park my BMW in between.

I do a quick check of my makeup and smooth my hair once more. I look cute. The weather is still quite cold, so I decided to wear a fitted, cashmere turtle neck, a pair of skinny cords, and my Tory Burch suede flats. As I'm locking my wallet in the glove compartment, I glance up at my new home and think about how wonderful our first dinner engagement will be.

I lock my car, and head up the grand entry. Each brick paver has been meticulously placed to accent the ornate limestone. The architectural detail that Rece has put into our home is unbelievable. Nothing has been missed. From the high-pitched roof to the keystones. Anyone that pulls up to our new home, will truly feel the essence and meaning of Renaissance.

Although Rece oversaw the design of the home, he has given majority of the project's control to an up and coming minority company. Wright Brothers Construction is owned and operated by two brothers, Joshua and Jacob Wright. Rece took a tour of some new properties downtown, and was so impressed by their work, that he decided to use them. Plus, he made arrangements for Devin to work with the brothers. So, it ended up being a win-win situation. I haven't met the brothers yet, but I'm excited by what I see so far.

The front door is open, and so I walk in and just take in the beauty of the double staircase. I truly love the dark wood and iron. I don't see anyone, but I hear some hammering and music coming from the kitchen. I head in that direction, but not before running my hand across one of the huge columns dividing the living and kitchen areas. I wonder how I am going to decorate this space. I was really hoping that Mom and Mrs. Gallantine would be a part of the process, but I guess that won't be happening. Shit!

As I step into the kitchen, I gasp at what I see before me. "Ohhh, my gosh! I love it! I love it!" I scream, before pouncing on top of my enormous center island. It is beyond fabulous. The imported granite, with hints of gray, muted gold, ivory and black, is to die for. I stretch out on the island, and just smile. I am going to make some mean desserts on this exquisite stone. I am so thrilled at the progress, and totally caught up in the moment, that I forgot that there are others in the house. It's not until I hear someone clearing their throat that I snap out of my daze, and sit straight up. As I look around, my eyes land on two of the most delectable, dark chocolate specimens I have ever seen in my entire life. When I say that Idris Alba and Morris Chestnut ain't got shit on these two brothas…whew! Damn it! Ooooh, Jesus! Bald, no facial or body hair, and ripped beyond measure.

"Uhh, I'm sorry." I manage to say, while reaching up to make sure my mouth is closed, and that I'm not drooling.

"Hi." They say in unison. Revealing perfectly white teeth. They are both shirtless, exposing what appears to be twelve packs. Each is sporting baggy, blue jeans, and I can see a hint of their plaid underwear. The taller of the two removes his tool belt and walks towards me extending his hand. I don't move. Not because I'm scared…I'm simply in awe.

"Hello, I'm Jacob Wright, and this is my brother, Joshua."

I quickly snap back into reality, "Oh, hi, gentlemen," I say, as I shake Jacob's hand. It's strong…callused. Joshua wipes his hands on his jeans and reaches for mine. Instead of shaking my hand, he holds it gently for what seems like a blissful eternity, and places a soft kiss on top. I feel an instant jolt of energy through my body. *What the fuck is happening?*

"My pleasure." He says. "You must be Mrs. Gallantine."

"Ummm, yes…yes, I am." I'm feeling flushed. *Damn it! What is wrong with me?*

"Here, let me help you down." Joshua lifts me, effortlessly, from the island. As my feet are nearing the floor, I feel our torsos slightly touch. He keeps his hands on my waist. "There." He says, with a slight air of flirtation. I take a step back to allow some space in between whatever the fuck is taking place right now.

Jacob reaches for his bottled water, and takes a sip. "So, I take it you like your new kitchen?" He asks, while leaning against the stainless steel refrigerator. The color of his deep chocolate skin against the steel is delightful…delicious.

"Yes, I do. I love it! It's actually better than I imagined." *Willow, are you really talking about the kitchen, or the men in the kitchen?* I find myself blushing, because Jacob is undressing me with his eyes. I clearly notice it, and he's not being shy about his intent. Joshua interjects, and asks me to come over to where he is standing so he can show me how to work my new gadgets. He hands me a small remote control. "This remote controls everything in here, from the temperature of your refrigerator, to the timers on your double ovens."

"Wow, this is cool." I reply.

"Now," taking my hand and placing it just beneath the remote, "do you feel that button?" Joshua asks, while leaning in closer. I can really smell him. He smells really clean. Having his hand on mine, along with his yummy scent, is causing butterflies to erupt in my stomach. I'm totally off guard. I barely manage to get out a breathy, "Yeah…I feel it."

"Well, this is the emergency button. Push it if you need to stop, or turn off anything in an instant. Okay?" He winks at me.

"Ummm, okay. I think I got it." I'm blushing uncontrollably, and I can't stop. I'm not quite sure where to land my eyes. To the right…heaven…to the left…divine. *Okay, Willow, you need to get it together. But, look at those abs, those arms, those lips…SHIT!*

"Wow! Mr. Gallantine is a lucky man. Where can a brother like me, find someone like you? I mean…damn!" Jacob says, before chuckling to himself.

I give him a quick stare down before stating, "I'm sure that a nice looking brother like you, doesn't have any problems in the dating department."

"Man," while running his hand down his abs, "you have no idea. It's a jungle out there."

They both laugh.

"I'm with you, bro, I never run into anything close to this, and if I do, it's usually some kinda drama attached. Crazy ex-boyfriend, or husband, or in this day and time… crazy ex-girlfriend."

We all laugh.

"I'm flattered gentlemen."

"Don't be, because it's the truth." Joshua licks his lips. I feel myself getting weak.

"How about we give you a tour?" Jacob asks, while reaching for my arm. I get a whiff of him. Mmmm, Versace

Eros. I let the brothers guide me through the living and formal dining room areas, before leading me down the hall into the master suite.

I can't contain my joy. The room is stunning. The carpet is installed, and the custom- wall unit that will house the television is awesome. Rece will be in heaven when he sees it. Our lovely, leather reading chairs have arrived for the sitting area. I can't wait to enjoy my morning cup of coffee in here.

As I am standing in the middle of the room trying to take in every bit of detail, I feel a hand on my lower back. It slightly startles me. I turn quickly. It's Jacob.

"I'm sorry." He says. "I didn't mean to scare you."

"Uhhh, I'm okay."

"Well, do you like?" He asks with pride.

"I like." *And I ain't talking about the damn room. Willow, pump your damn brakes girl! I knew I shouldn't have had that glass of wine before coming here. Wine always makes me hot and horny. Now, I'm standing in between these two African kings, and everything inside of me is going crazy. I keep seeing flashes of the night on the plane, and how incredible it was to be pleasured by two women. But, what about two men? NO, WILLOW…don't even go there!*

"Well, guys, I think I'm gonna get on outta here." I say, unconvincingly.

"So soon?" Joshua inquires.

"Yeah, I better go before I…uhh."

"What? What is it?" Jacob asks.

I take a deep breath. "Okay, here I go. Joshua and Jacob, I find the two of you incredibly sexy. I mean…shit! I'm newly married. I love my husband, but…"

"But what, Mrs. Gallantine?" Jacob grabs my hand, but this time he doesn't let go.

"Willow…my name is Willow." I exhale, and look down at the floor. Jacob lifts my chins. "But what?"

I take a really deep breath, and just blurt it out. "I want to fuck the both of you! There, I said it."

"Shit, you ain't said nothing. I wanted you as soon as I saw you." Jacob says, without shame and with complete confidence.

"But, you don't understand guys, I'm married!" I throw my arms up.

Joshua steps in front of me, and places his fingers over my lips. "Shhh, we got you, baby girl." I feel Jacob removing my sweater. I don't put up a fight. Joshua slips off my boots and cord jeans. I find myself standing in between two brothers in only my bra and thong.

"Fuck!" Joshua exclaims, after removing my bra. Jacob slides my thong off and brings it up to his nose. He sniffs and sniffs, again, before saying, "Heaven…simply heaven."

Jacob turns me around and kisses me hard. His tongue tastes good. His mouth is molten hot…intoxicating. I eagerly unzip Jacob's jeans to reveal his hardened, chocolate masterpiece. I feel Joshua massaging my ass, and then I feel him spreading my thighs apart so he can insert a finger into my tunnel of love. I shudder with delight. Joshua plays a melodic tune on my G-spot, before stopping to undress. What he exposes when he removes his jeans, is beyond. I can't even find the words to describe it. It's a work of art. Joshua lies down on the floor, and pulls me down onto his face. While he delights my kitty, I grab Jacob's dick and begin to blow a slow, soft, down home bluesy tune.

What happens for the next hour will never be spoken of again…

Printed in the United States
By Bookmasters